Shadowwraith

A Novel of Sherlock Holmes

Tracy Revels

Published in the UK by MX Publishing
335 Princess Park Manor, Royal Drive, London, N11 3GX
www.mxpublishing.co.uk

Cover artwork by www.staunch.com

For Dr. Dwain Pruitt

(Who said, "Make it Darker.")

Also from Tracy Revels

Shadowfall

"This is a comforting and disquieting book all at the same time. The sense of `1895' is so strong that it overwhelms the strangeness introduced by the preternatural elements for most of the narrative. Holmes and Watson work together with the familiar combination of trust and knowledge that fill the Canon but are finally separated by their own natures and circumstances. It is odd and familiar, comfortable and unsettling. It is just, as I suppose, as the author planned it to be."

Philip K Jones.

Shadowblood

"The sequel to "Shadowfall" is just as deliriously weird. "Shadowblood" by Tracy Revels introduces us again to the World of Shadows, whose interaction with our own world can be devastating. Watson's recuperation from his previous encounters with the supernatural is interrupted when an unpleasant recluse demands that Holmes find his missing daughter. Shortly after the detective's arrival, the old man is horribly murdered, and Holmes's own Shadowborn powers are tested to the limit in a quest for the girl and, ultimately, for the Fountain of Youth. He and Watson travel to Prague, where they are helped by Dr John Dee, and then to St Augustine, Florida, where they receive assistance and opposition from even stranger beings. The missing girl is practising blood magic and has acquired a very dangerous assistant, a woman skilled in murder. I said that "Shadowfall" is rather like an enjoyable nightmare. "Shadowblood" is even more enjoyable."

The Sherlock Holmes Society of London

Prologue

This is a story that the world will never read. I write it, my Lady, for your eyes alone and at your request.

I have tried, to the best of my ability, to be truthful about the events that followed our return from America. I am giving you my thoughts and feelings, even at the risk of some embarrassment on my part. You have asked me to be forthright, to hold nothing back, to craft my tale naturally. I have done my best to be observant of your instruction.

These days I have described were among the darkest and most dangerous that I have ever experienced while in the company of Sherlock Holmes. We owe you a great debt, and in these pages I hope that I may, in part, repay mine.

I remain, as always, your devoted servant and deepest admirer.

John H. Watson, M.D

Chapter One

"Mr. Holmes, do you believe in ghosts?"

A young lady in a cornflower blue dress posed the question. Her silly straw hat, perched atop her tousled golden hair, bobbled with barely suppressed anxiety. There was nothing but innocence in her worried expression and naivety in her open, bright gaze. Her inquiry rose upward in pitch, like the hopeful twitter of a small bird. Sherlock Holmes considered her for a long moment, amusement lightening his eyes. Had a man asked the question, or had the inquiry been spoken by a woman of lesser charms, I had no doubt he would have scoffed or perhaps gestured toward the door, ending the consultation. But for this enchanting creature, he only smiled.

"The world is big enough for us," he said, with the gentleness of a nanny to a distressed infant. "No ghosts need apply."

"Then how does a spirit leave me gifts every night?" our visitor asked. "And how can a message of love appear on my pillow, in my dead darling's very own handwriting?"

I reached for my notebook. It appeared that Miss Beatrice Simone had a problem Holmes would find intriguing. I was grateful for this unusual diversion, for Holmes had been complaining of boredom since our return from America just two weeks before and, as always, I feared the effects of any prolonged bout of ennui upon the complex machinery of his remarkable mind.

"This sounds like a most exceptional revenant," Holmes agreed, and only one who had known him as long as I had would have noted the change in his tone or the subtle way he shifted in his chair. He placed his hands together, his long white fingers forming a steeple. Despite the dreamy lassitude that marked his features, I was aware that Miss Simone's story now claimed his full attention. "But if you will, please begin at the beginning," he instructed.

The lady looked to me, eyebrows lifted in delicate and endearing confusion. I nodded encouragement to her, and she stiffened her back, clutching a frayed velvet reticule in her lap.

"When I speak of my life and of the loved one I have lost, I hope you will not judge me too harshly, Mr. Holmes."

"I assure you, Madame, that I have made the acquaintance of men and women in all circles of society. I do not consider an artist's model to be in any way an inferior person."

Miss Simone started. "You know me, then?"

"I know of you," he corrected, "for I have seen your image. As have you, Doctor. Do you not recall *Nymph amid Flowers* or *Diana and Her Maidens* in the Regent Street galleries?"

This reminder raised color in my cheeks. I had thought the lady looked somewhat familiar when she entered our sitting room, and now I understood why. I had seen her face, and indeed almost all of her unclad form, romping about in a series of rather pedestrian canvases that the *Times* had denounced as 'a poor attempt at Pre-Raphaelite mimicry.' The lady put pink-gloved fingers to her lips.

"It is true, I have been a model for almost five years and I have posed for a number of artists. Most of them treated me as little better than a woman of the streets and made the most improper advances, which I was sometimes forced to fend off with nothing more than a paper harp or a basket of wax fruit. But everything changed a year ago when Mr. Robert Smythe engaged me to pose for him."

Holmes interrupted gently. "Would this artist be Mr. Robert *Vernet* Smythe, by any chance?"

"Yes! You know him?"

"By reputation only," Holmes allowed.

Our visitor's face colored a bit, and an edge of defensiveness sharpened her words. "Then you know he is a very *kind* gentleman---proper, with lovely manners, and honorable intentions. Unfortunately, he is also quite penniless. He promised marriage and I accepted, even though we had no money to begin our lives together in an honest fashion."

"And what strange commission did he accept, in order to obtain the funds to make your arrangement more respectable?" Holmes asked.

The lady frowned. "You seem to know the story already."

Holmes waggled one hand. "All stories have been told before. They follow along certain well-travelled roads and I can usually predict where the carriage of the narrative will turn. But please, continue."

She gave him a petulant look and resumed. "A month ago, Mr. Smythe---*Robert*---came to me in great excitement. He had been commissioned to paint a portrait of a very famous man. I begged him to tell me more, but he said he had been sworn to secrecy. He also told me that he would have to go to Reading and be in residence at his patron's house until the painting was completed." She paused, clearly struggling with her emotions. She swallowed tightly. Her eyes filled with tears. "I presume you know what happened next."

Holmes shook his head. Miss Simone's hands clenched.

"I received a telegram. There was no name attached to it---it was signed only as 'a friend'---but it told me that my darling had been killed in the great fire at Urian Hall. The blaze was in the papers, but since I had never known the place or the name I could not..."

Miss Simone lost her composure, bursting into sobs. As I did my best to console her, Holmes leaned over

8

and shuffled through the debris near his feet. He had been updating his index earlier that morning and clippings were scattered everywhere.

"'Horrible explosion at Urian Hall,'" Holmes read aloud, quickly summarizing the story. "The conflagration was blamed on faulty gas lines. Several people were killed, but the bodies were unidentified."

Miss Simone nodded, daubing a handkerchief to her cheek. "I went to Reading and viewed the remains, but...there was no way to know which, if any, of those poor corpses was Robert. And nothing remained of the house. It had been reduced to ashes. When a week passed and I did not hear from him, I was certain. He was gone."

"And you never learned who sent the telegram?" I asked. Even as the question dropped from my lips, I heard Holmes give a sharp snort, as if I had just made the most asinine inquiry imaginable. Fortunately, the lady did not notice, and merely whispered 'no' in reply.

"When did the gifts begin to appear?" Holmes asked.

"Three weeks ago. I would awaken and find coins on my nightstand---shillings at first, then sovereigns. I thought these were from my landlady, who had taken such pity on me, but when I thanked her for her kindness she denied that the gifts were her doing. And then, last week, a stickpin set with garnets appeared, followed by a strand of pearls. You cannot imagine how it frightened me, to awake to such trophies. I was prepared to flee my rooms, lest I be accused of thievery, but this morning I found a note on the pillow where my darling used to lay his head. I have it here."

She opened her purse and passed a small slip of paper to Holmes. He glanced at it and thrust it at me. Out of habit, I read it aloud.

"Beloved Venus, do not leave. I am caring for you. Wait and pray. RVS."

"Venus was his pet name for me," Miss Simone said, lowering her gaze. "And that is his handwriting, I would swear it on my life."

"Is it possible that this could be some kind of elaborate hoax?" I asked. The lady turned and glared at me. Hurriedly, I tried to amend the directness of my statement. "I only mean that artists are often possessed of strange temperaments. Could he be---"

"Testing your fidelity?" Holmes finished, as I futilely attempted to stammer an apology.

"No, he would never do such a thing," Miss Simone snapped. "And there is only one door to my room. Since Robert's death I have added a deadbolt to it, and new latches to the window as well. My chamber is on third floor, not even an acrobat could reach it. And yet all of these things have appeared!" With trembling hands, she upended the reticule and a small fortune in jewelry tumbled across her skirts. Pearls, rubies, garnets and even diamonds winked up at us. "What on earth should I do? If Robert is not dead, how does he gain access to my room? And why will he not wake me and reveal himself to me?"

"You parted on good terms?" Holmes asked.

"The best," Miss Simone said, as she gathered up the gems and passed the collection to Holmes for his examination. "He promised that once he had been paid for his secret commission, we would go to the church and be married."

I pretended to take a great interest in my notes. While I could not account for the manner in which the jewels and the letter were left in the lady's room, it was easy enough to imagine the reasoning behind them, especially as I considered the color of her face and the way her hand fluttered protectively over her bodice.

"He would not leave me," Miss Simone said, with sudden desperation in her voice, as if she had read my thoughts. "But I do not know where to turn."

"Did your fiancé have a previous commission for Lord Whiteleigh?" Holmes asked. The lady was as startled by the question as I was.

"I think...yes. Now I remember! He told me last year he painted the Lord's favorite hunting dog. Or was it his wife?"

Holmes smirked. "I have seen both and the confusion is understandable." He returned the finery to Miss Simone, except for a small broach. "If you will allow me to retain this item, it will assist me in my investigation."

"Then you will help me! You will find Robert's ghost!"

Holmes waved airily. "My dear lady, I will find your fiancé in the flesh. And when I do, I will chastise him soundly for playing a dastardly trick on such a lovely sweetheart. However, I will need one further object in order to conduct my inquiry."

With that announcement, Holmes rose and tore a scrap of paper from my notebook, ignoring my look of annoyance at the mutilation of my property. He scribbled a few words on the page and passed it to the lady. She read the message and gasped.

"How did you know it was there?"

"Because it had to be there," Holmes replied. "Send it to me as quickly as you can."

Miss Simone departed with a hopeful expression and trembling lips. I went to the window, waiting until I could see her magnificent figure, crowned by her ridiculous hat, bobbing through the crowd on Baker Street.

"Really, Holmes, that was unkind of you," I reprimanded. My friend joined me at the window, blue smoke trailing from his pipe.

"How do you mean, Watson?"

"Promising the girl that you could find her fellow! Clearly he is either dead or, if he has somehow faked his death, anxious to be rid of her."

"Come now, Watson! Why would a man go to such lengths to break into a locked room and deposit money and gemstones on his paramour's bedside table, if he no longer loved her?"

"A guilty conscience, perhaps?"

Holmes gave a dry chuckle. "I confess that I may have a certain advantage in grasping the truth of this matter."

"As you always do," I answered. "For instance--- how did you know Smythe had a commission from Lord Whiteleigh?"

"That required no great powers of deduction, but merely a sound knowledge of British heraldry." Holmes pulled the broach from his pocket and held it to the light. "You see the arrows and the four falcons? The crest is distinctive."

"Stolen! So Smythe is a thief as well as a coward."

"Or, perhaps, a rather hopeless romantic. It will be interesting to put the question to the man himself."

"And when do you expect to interview him?" I asked with a huff.

"He will be in these rooms as of..."

Holmes ceased speaking. He put his pipe on the windowsill, waving away the smoke. I was about to question this unusual behavior when, quite suddenly, I understood its purpose.

There was a new odor in the air, one that was rapidly overcoming the scent of burning tobacco. It was pungent; not unpleasant, but very strong, as if a hundred roses had suddenly been delivered to our suite, all of them exploding in full bloom. I stared at Holmes, whose substantial nostrils were quivering.

"Yes, Watson, it does smell like a funeral in here," he said. "I think it is safe to deduce that we have an unannounced guest."

Chapter Two

Slowly, we both turned from the window. I was astonished to see a figure draped in brown cloth, with a dark hood covering its head, standing like sentinel in the far corner of the room. I cast a quick glance at Holmes, who seemed initially as perplexed as I. How could anyone, especially an individual so encumbered by long robes, have entered our chamber without causing a sound? Only the day before, Holmes had complained about the creaking of the door and suggested to Mrs. Hudson that she oil the rusty hinges, an action I knew very well our good landlady had not yet performed.

I was poised to speak when my friend's expression altered, giving him the look of a man who has suddenly remembered where to find a misplaced item.

"Of course, I should have known immediately from the scent! You will never be a most efficient criminal, Blessed One," Holmes said with a chuckle. "The odor of sanctity gives you away."

The apparition stepped forward, lifting its cowl. The action revealed a diminutive, matronly woman in the brown habit of a nun, with a white wimple framing her face. She smiled at us and spoke playfully, with a strong Italian accent.

"But I do so like---how is it that you say?---'burgling' my way into a building. It was how I made them take me into the order. I simply burgled my way inside the convent walls, appearing as if from the very air, like a miracle, until the good sisters were convinced they had to accept me as one of their own."

She moved closer and the smell of roses grew even stronger, as if emanating from her frame. I took in more details about her, which only added to my confusion. Her skin looked old and leathery, dried as if it had been hanging in a tanner's yard, yet her teeth were shockingly bright. There was a deep wound on her forehead and bare, crinkled feet protruded from the hem of her simple gown. Most perplexing, however, was the complete lack of her right eyebrow, and the sagging quality of her right cheek, which gave the appearance of an unhealed fracture beneath the skin.

To add to my confusion, Holmes offered her a reverent bow.

"Welcome to my home, Blessed One. It has been a long time since we last met." He extended a hand toward me. "This is my good friend and colleague, Dr. John Watson. Doctor, I have the honor of presenting Saint Rita of Cascia, Patroness of Impossible Causes."

My befuddlement grew deeper. "A living saint?" I whispered, with some skepticism. Holmes's lips twitched; he was clearly enjoying my plight.

"Not living," Holmes said. "Dead. But incorruptible."

I stared. I hope I may be forgiven for my reaction. After having met wizards and witches, conjurers and a voodoo loa, not to mention a cursed, skeletal conquistador and the queen of the fairies, I should have taken an introduction to such a fantastic character as an undead saint in stride. But being told that I was in the presence of a walking, talking impossibility---who was likewise a figure of passionate devotion among the Catholic faithful---was still shocking and nearly incomprehensible. I found myself reeling backward, clutching at the windowsill for support.

"Steady on," Holmes chided. "Saint Rita is on our side. Please, good lady, be seated."

The figure shook her head. "I cannot stay. In Cascia, there is always a chance that a pious soul will enter the chapel and note my absence from my crystal casket. I must be brief."

I caught Holmes by the arm. "How did you make the acquaintance of a saint?"

The nun answered instead. "Mr. Holmes was good enough to solve a mystery concerning some relics stolen from my church. They are now safely ensconced in Rome."

"The Vatican cameos," Holmes said, in a quick aside to me, "I will tell you the story someday." He freed himself from my grasp, picked up his pipe and walked to the mantel. "Blessed One, I know you have not crossed the heavenly plane and returned to your corporeal form merely to exchange pleasantries. How may I serve you?"

The saint folded her hands. With each movement, no matter how discreet, the aroma of roses grew stronger. I could scarcely breathe amid the heady sweetness that filled the air.

"You know my story, Mr. Holmes, of how I prayed for the death of my own sons rather than to allow them to murder the men who killed their father. For this reason I am most sensitive to revenge in any form. I weep in paradise when vendettas are waged. But this time, I cannot be content to merely mourn and plead my case with the angels. Instead I am taking action."

"So two sweet ladies have sought my aid in one afternoon," Holmes mused. "This is most unusual."

The saint's leathery skin puckered into a frown. "I am not seeking your aid, Mr. Holmes. Rather, I have come to warn you. The dead of Palermo have begun to whisper."

Holmes frowned, once again seeming to be puzzled by her simple words. "The dead are whispering? So tell me, what do they discuss?"

The saint's wimple rattled with her quick shake of her head. "Their words are not clear. But they are agitated and anxious."

Holmes accepted this information with a solemn nod. "There is no more you can tell me?"

"Only that they have been uneasy for almost a month." She pressed her hands together in an attitude of prayer. "Today, I thought I heard your name in their profane mutterings and thus it was decided. I had to warn you. I should have come sooner."

"My dear lady, you should not have come at all," Holmes replied. "While I appreciate your concern, you must know that danger is part of my business. I expect assault by evil forces on an hourly basis."

The saint sighed. "So will not listen to my pleas?"

"On the contrary, I will listen and be watchful, even more diligent than before. I value your concern, but I regret that you felt the need to make such an arduous journey."

"Oh, but I have enjoyed it," the lady said, and humor returned to her eyes. "I have wanted for some time to visit your rooms---and what I see is that you need a good wife, to keep them clean for you! Should you not reconsider the blessings of matrimony, Mr. Holmes?"

It clearly required all of my friend's formidable self-control not to laugh at her suggestion. "Mine would hardly be a proper life for a spouse to share, as you have noted. I would never willingly expose a woman to such peril."

The saint looked toward me. Her single eyebrow rose in question. I coughed and hoped that I did not sound ludicrous in my reply.

"I choose to share these dangers willingly, my good lady."

The saint gave a motherly shrug. "Then there is nothing more I can do. I will return my body to its crystal coffin and my soul to heaven...though when I place my mortal flesh back in its casket, I will shift my old bones around a bit! The faithful do enjoy that so!" She raised a hand in blessing and farewell. "*Arrivederci*, Mr. Holmes, Dr. Watson. May God bless you and protect you."

To my amazement, the saint began to fade, the brown and white of her habit leeching to dull beige. Her outline became indistinct, and then, by degrees, transparent. Likewise the aroma of roses began to soften, till there was nothing but a breath of fragrance in the air. I blinked, and the lady had completely vanished, taking her perfume with her.

"My word," I whispered. "Was she truly a saint, or one of your Shadow creatures?"

Holmes moved to the index and pulled down a volume. He laid a finger upon an entry beneath a grainy photograph. The picture showed a body in a glass box. I read the pertinent details of the article aloud.

"Saint Rita of Cascia...married to a cruel husband...converted him to Christianity...entered an Augustinian convent...died 1472! Beatified in 1600."

"Not yet officially canonized," Holmes remarked, "though I suspect that long delayed event will take place shortly. As you can tell, she both was and is a very remarkable woman."

"And the evil spirits that she warned you of? The whispering dead?"

Holmes shrugged and returned the book to the shelf. "Wicked shades are called from the dead on a regular basis." He paused, his hand still resting on the book's spine. "But why would Italian spirits be using my name? Especially from Palermo, in Sicily? While my practice has taken me across Europe, and it is true that I have put an end to a few notable Italian criminals in the mafia and other secret societies, I can recall no one---living or dead---from Palermo who should bear me any ill-will. However..."

I found his silence tantalizing. "Go on."

Holmes's face was suddenly drawn and troubled. "There are lines of power in the Earth, places where the walls between Sun and Shadow, as well as between Heaven and Hell, are weakened. Palermo sits on a crossroads. Anyone looking to do mischief to the world would be hard pressed to choose a better place, a location where power flows erratically and portals between realities may be opened."

"So you will go there?" I asked, expecting Holmes to order me to pack my bags immediately and consult the Bradshaw for our trains.

"No---I have no desire for an Italian holiday!" Holmes laughed. "Also, I find Miss Simone's case more appealing. Let the dead in Palermo whisper. If they wish my attention, they must speak more clearly!"

"Shall I come with you?"

"I think not, Watson." Holmes retreated to his room for his coat, returning in an instant, his features alight with excitement, as eager as a hound at the sound of the hunter's horn. "I think I may move faster and more efficiently if unencumbered."

My face surely expressed my dislike of being so cavalierly dismissed from service. Holmes took note of my scowl and folded arms.

"I did not mean for you to infer that you are not wanted, Watson, for I need you to perform a far more pleasant task!"

"Oh? And what might that be?"

Holmes went to his desk and removed an envelope. "Here are two tickets to tonight's performance at the Lyceum Theatre, and a note from a potential client asking for my assistance. Will you consent to be my proxy in this matter?"

"Holmes, I could hardly hope to--"

He slapped the envelope into my hand and clapped me on the shoulder. "There's a good fellow. I shall expect a full report in the morning!"

With a burst of energy, he was gone from the room before I could even inquire as to the client's name.

Chapter Three

Later that evening, I donned suitable attire and hailed a cab. I had spent the afternoon half dozing, having failed to find any excitement in the yellow backed novels that lay scattered about the room. As the vehicle made its way toward the Lyceum Theatre I could not help but reflect on a previous journey to that same destination with Holmes and my darling Mary. I closed my eyes and momentarily lost myself to the remembered scent of her perfume, the feel of her small hand pressed to mine as we embarked on that strange and dangerous case that began with the yearly delivery of a pearl and ended with a fatal chase along the Thames. Holmes had solved the mystery, but it was I who won a prize greater than the Agra treasure when the lovely Mary Morstan agreed to become my wife. No man had ever loved a more beautiful or devoted spouse.

A sudden, rough jolt of the cab brought back the memories of my beloved's final, painful days, as she sank deeper into the throes of consumption. I recalled her labored breath and bloody cough. I had done all that I could; I carried her to every specialist in England, and dozens more on the continent, but none could bring her relief, much less a cure. Thunder echoed in my mind, and I was once more standing beside her grave at Kensal Green, with rain pouring all around me.

I shook my head and sought to banish my darkness. I glanced down at the note that accompanied the tickets.

'I would much appreciate your professional advice on the matter of the fraud being perpetuated at the Lyceum. Sincerely, JNM.'

Of course, Holmes had not prepared me for the meeting. I knew nothing more than the initials of my evening's companion. I permitted myself a moment of vexation with Holmes and, for the final blocks of the journey, indulged a fantasy of how my life might have been if I had never met him, or if I had taken up lodgings with Stamford instead.

At last I descended the cab and paid the driver. The show would begin in only ten minutes, and a great wave of fashionable citizenry was crashing over the theatre's historic steps. There was more than the usual murmur of excitement in the well-dressed throng. I looked back at the words printed on my ticket. 'Professor Steele's Historical Monologues' hardly sounded like a crowd-pleaser to me.

"Good evening, Dr. Watson."

I turned. A tall, thin gentleman stood beside me. He wore evening clothes with such ease that one might assume he was born in them, and his dark eyes caught and held mine with a hypnotic force. Though his heavy mustache seemed almost comical on such a pale face, I had no courage to laugh, as his entire bearing commanded obedience. I immediately felt that I knew him, but I could not think of why. Though Holmes's cases had made us both public figures, I still found it somewhat disconcerting to be hailed by a stranger, even one that seemed so oddly familiar. The gentleman extended a gloved hand.

"I take it Mr. Holmes is unable to attend tonight's performance?"

I murmured an apology, explaining that a previous case had taken a dramatic turn. Much to my relief, the man expressed no displeasure at the substitution, but merely gave a stoic shrug and gestured for us to join the crowd entering the lobby.

"I am grateful for your assistance, Doctor. After your long association with Mr. Holmes, no doubt you have learned his methods."

I demurred and allowed that he had me at such a disadvantage that I did not even know his name. Before he could answer, a little boy broke away from his parents and ran over to my companion. The child danced with delight, demanding an autograph. The gentleman consented with a benevolent smile, and after signing his name to the back of a ticket he pulled a shilling from the boy's ear.

I at last knew him. "You are the Great Maskelyne!"

I had found myself in the company of John Nevil Maskelyne, London's reigning stage magician. There was no finer conjurer anywhere in the empire. I felt something like a schoolboy myself, but I forced my curiosity down to a more mature level. I longed to quiz him as to how he made beautiful damsels float in mid-air, but doubted that he would tell me. Had Holmes himself not warned me that magicians received no credit if they explained their illusions?

"You mentioned a fraud," I said, as we were shown to box seats.

"Yes. Perhaps you have read that I have made something of a career of exposing mediums that claim to talk with the dead and offer magicians' tricks as their proof. I have no quarrel with any conjurer, as long as he makes it clear that his tricks are just that---a clever bit of misdirection, a subtle slight of hand. People pay willingly to be deceived for entertainment, and as such the magical profession is an ancient and honorable one. It is the bloodsuckers who rob the purses of the bereaved, by dishonest means, that I abhor."

I had often heard Holmes speak the same way. I recalled an evening when he had regaled me with a recitation of Maskelyne's success as an investigator of crimes against naïve mourners who sought solace only to have their grief cruelly manipulated for profit. Holmes clearly considered Maskelyne a fellow detective and a champion of justice.

"But this show presents me with a strange quandary," my companion continued. "I do not wish to prejudice you in advance, however. Let us watch it together and discuss it afterward."

The house lights dimmed. There was a round of applause as the great velvet curtain rose. I reminded myself that I must pay attention, be able to repeat all the details of the evening to Holmes in order to be judged a loyal and trustworthy partner.

A lone figure stood on the bare stage. It was a woman of ponderous girth, so stout she could easily have qualified for inclusion in a circus sideshow, her bulk made even more ridiculous by the heavy scholar's gown she wore and the mortarboard that sat askew atop her frizzled red curls. She introduced herself as Professor Suzanna Steele, of the Women's Seminary in Charleston, South Carolina. In a voice mellow with the rich vowels of the American South, she described her childhood in the romantic city and how she lost her only suitor to a rival. Despondent over her fate, she had thrown herself into Charleston harbor. Rescued and revived, she found she was possessed of a new talent: the ability to call ghosts from their graves.

"But I am no medium, no spiritualist," she assured her audience, which had begun to grow restless with her stilted dialogue. "I am a lover of history, a worshipper at the feet of the muse Clio. I would not be stingy with my gift and so, dear friends, I present to you my collection of the famous dead. Their stories are, I freely admit, more interesting than my own!"

The gaslights dimmed further as the lady waddled from the stage. The crowd began to murmur and then, with a great explosion of red smoke, a toga-clad man appeared in the exact spot the lady had vacated. He wore an olive branch crown on his thick curls and sandals on his feet. He strode forward and raised his hand, authority and determination radiating from every pore.

"I am Julius Caesar," he proclaimed.

I pulled my opera glasses from my pocket. My eyes had not deceived me. The man seemed real and solid. He even breathed in a regular fashion.

Yet he was simultaneously transparent. I could see through him, as if he were made of coloured glass.

He began to speak in a booming baritone voice. He told of battles and campaigns, of conquering Gaul and fighting blue-painted barbarians in Britain. His stories were compelling, and one soon forgot the astonishing quality of his appearance. I pulled my program from my pocket, squinting in the darkness, searching in vain for the performer's name.

A shriek took me back to the stage. The actor had begun to stagger and clutch at his garments. Dark fountains of blood spouted from his chest and shoulders. He gave a cry and tumbled to his knees, as more scarlet fluid poured from his body. He lifted his face, his whole countenance consumed in agony.

"*Et tu, Brute?*" he wailed. "Then die, Caesar!"

He fell, full length, his final motion the languid lifting of one bleeding arm to pull a fold of his toga over his face. There was spellbound silence, followed by wild applause. The man on the stage faded and vanished.

"Astounding!" I said, adding my own clapping to the din below us. "Tell me, what did you think?"

Maskelyne did not answer and it was too dim to see his face.

"And now," Professor Steele's voice called, from the wings, "I give you Marie Antoinette."

Another explosion brought forth the famous French queen in all her bewigged and bejeweled glory. Rubies, sapphires, and diamonds winked in her ornate gown, while her coiffure rose nearly a yard above her head. Despite the outrageous attire, there was a trace of girlish beauty and naivety about her, which shown like a beacon. One could admire her celebrated beauty even from the rafters of the theater.

Her voice was soft, but still it carried. In passionate whispers, she told of her many dashing and adventurous lovers. She spoke of the ignorance of the French peasants, and her laughter tinkled like fine glass when she described how she informed the poor people that, if they had no bread, they should eat cake. The audience laughed with her. Abruptly, even as her listeners still chuckled, the queen began to cower and scream. She dropped to the stage, her arms pulled away from her body, held back by invisible assailants.

"No! *Messieurs*, have mercy! Please! I did not mean to do it!"

Suddenly, as if a spectral blade had fallen, her head flew from her body and rolled across the floor, coming to rest just in the illumination of the footlights. Black blood slowly pooled around the now headless corpse. I noted with horror that the lady's eyes were still blinking, her lips moving in a silent plea.

The curtain dropped with a thunderous crash. There was an instant of stunned silence, and then applause erupted once more.

For the next two hours, we were treated to stories from the heroes of history, each of whom had each come to a tragic or horrifying end. We saw Richard III cut down in battle, Abraham Lincoln assassinated, and Joan of Arc burned at the stake. There was no intermission, only the rise and fall of the curtain, and yet the audience never wavered or abandoned their seats. The concluding actor portrayed Thomas Beckett, and he pronounced a blessing on us immediately before unseen knights attacked him, driving him to the floor of an imagined Canterbury Cathedral. The audience surged to its feet. Roses were tossed to the stage as the lady professor came forward to take a solo bow. At last the house lights returned. While still staring at the curtain, my companion asked my opinion.

"Astonishing!" I answered. "I have never seen anything like it."

"Indeed," the magician said dryly. "I had thought our British audiences above such performances of the *Grand Guignol* type, but I see I have misjudged my peers."

"How was it achieved? I presume it is some type of magic trick."

"It should be a modern example of a *phantasmagoria*," he said dryly. "A production in which specters, created by projections on cloth or on smoke, are summoned for entertainment. This type of show was popular almost a century ago. Indeed, at first appearance, the 'professor's' performance is nothing more sensational than a clever use of Pepper's Ghost."

"What do you mean?"

Maskelyne rubbed his pale fingers against his mustache. "Pepper's ghost is a technique by which 'spirits' may be raised to interact with actors. Simply put, there is a projector beneath the stage, which casts the image of a sheet-draped figure onto a large pane of glass. What the audience sees is a reflection, but they can not tell it is a mere illusion because the glass, which bears the image, is angled away from the seats."

I looked back to the stage. "It was a remarkable feat."

"Too remarkable," my companion said. "I have never seen a performance with such natural coloring and action. And there is another problem as well."

"What is that?" I asked.

"I have been below the stage during the performance, Doctor. I have been below, above, and to the side." He turned, casting a mournful, dark gaze on me. "And the thing is impossible...for there is no projector and no glass."

Chapter Four

I returned home just as the bells across London were striking one. The Great Maskelyne had treated me to a late supper and amused me with many tales of his adventures on both the stage and in the underworld of the mediums and fraudulent spiritualists. I thought that should Holmes dismiss me as his biographer, I could construct an equally entertaining series of vignettes of this sorcerer's life. I even entertained the idea of making such a threat, for my friend Sherlock Holmes, despite his cold and seeming unflinching nature, had a deep streak of jealousy. He was vain about his own gifts and not overly eager to see them applauded in others, unless he was doing the applauding.

Holmes was still away, however, and after falling asleep twice in my chair and awakening with a most uncomfortable cramp in my neck, I gave up my vigil and retired. There was no sign of him at daybreak, and Mrs. Hudson gave a shake of her head when I asked if he had returned.

"Indeed he has not, though a package came for him last evening. I put it over there, by the fireplace."

"Do you know what is in it?" I asked.

"Good heavens, do you think I would sneak a look at anything that arrived for Mr. Holmes? It could be some kind of poisonous snake, or a bloodstained shirt, or a severed hand!"

I conceded that Holmes's mail was a singularly unpredictable thing and praised our gracious landlady for her wisdom before turning my attention to breakfast.

Several uneventful hours passed. I was just finishing my luncheon coffee when the door of the sitting room flew open and Holmes gestured to me for assistance. I found that he was struggling with a number of large, paper-wrapped parcels.

"You have been shopping," I noted.

"Collecting, to be more precise," Holmes said as we carried the items into the room and propped them against the sofa. "I am fortunate that our missing artist is young, otherwise I might have had more difficulty gathering up his oeuvre."

With that announcement, Holmes began ripping the paper free. With my help, six painted canvases were soon revealed. Giving a little cry of delight, Holmes opened the package that had arrived the night before. Within it was a seventh, smaller painting. Holmes stepped back, considering the artwork with the look of a connoisseur.

"What do you make of them, Watson?"

I commented that I found the paintings rather dull. Four were pastoral scenes and might have come from any journeyman's brush. One was a study of a country churchyard, done in the style of the Impressionists, and the other a stylized portrait of a noblewoman. Her jowls sagged and her eyes were at odd angles in her face; she was either the most hideous woman on earth or proof of the artist's overwhelming lack of talent. Holmes nodded in her direction.

"Lady Whiteleigh. I do believe our friend would have had more success had his subject been the nobleman's favorite canine." Holmes winked playfully. "When I inquired about purchasing it, Lord Whiteleigh offered to pay me to take 'that abomination' away. The other pieces I found in disreputable galleries where I paid no more than two quid apiece for them. I fear young Robert does no credit to my good family name."

"Your family?" I asked, but even as I spoke a memory returned. "Your grandmother---"

"Was a sister of the artist Vernet. This man is family, and art in the blood is liable to take the strangest forms, especially when that blood has the black tint of the Shadows."

"He has magical powers?"

"Indeed. His mode of transportation has not suggested itself to you?" Holmes smiled down at me, and I suddenly felt like the dullest child in school.

"I presume it has something to do with these pictures or you would not have gone to the trouble to collect them. But I cannot imagine what you are driving at."

Holmes pointed to the painting that had arrived the previous evening, telling me that it had come from

Miss Simone's lodgings. It was an unmemorable offering of a meadow strewn with daisies. He then gestured to the other pictures. "Watson, what do they have in common?"

"Besides being dreadful?"

"Yes."

I crouched and examined each painting. Ten minutes later, neither my knees nor my eyes could take the torture. I rose, shaking my head.

"They are all signed by the artist in the lower right hand corner. Otherwise I see no real connection."

Holmes's expression made it clear that I had missed a significant detail. "Watson, how many show human figures in the scene?"

"The portrait does and...is that supposed to be a man standing in the cemetery of the churchyard? It is difficult to tell."

Holmes lifted the indicated work. "A rather shadowy character, wouldn't you say? Very well, let us begin with it. If you would be so good as to stoke up the fire?"

I blinked for a moment, wondering if I had heard him correctly. At his nod, I moved to obey his unusual command. With a loud crack, Holmes removed the canvas from its frame and tossed the artwork atop the blaze. The flames licked greedily at the picture. Holmes considered the burning image.

"I see my relative chooses to be obstinate. Very well. If you will hand me his next masterpiece?"

I picked up another of the country scenes. Holmes took it from me, studied it, and tapped a spot in the center.

There was a figure in it, standing atop a hill. I would have sworn that I had not seen that suggestion of a human presence before. I started to speak, but at that moment Holmes added the picture to the fire. It caught even faster than its predecessor, curling and crackling.

"Perhaps the portrait now, Watson?"

I raised it and studied it carefully. To my astonishment I saw the image of someone behind the lady, at a distance, like a servant peering around a doorway. Holmes merely hummed when I pointed it out to him. At his signal, I put it in the fire. The next three canvases were eliminated the same way, as Holmes shook his head.

"I dislike this destruction, but he forces me to it. Watson, add the final painting."

"But that is the one that belonged to Miss Simone." I was struck by how deeply the lady would grieve if we removed the last traces of her lover. "She will be bereft."

"I think she would prefer the man to his works. Watson, look at the picture."

I glanced down at the painting in my hand. A man now stood amid the field of daisies. His form was clear. He was a handsome chap, clad in the traditional artist's garb of a smock and paint-stained trousers, with a red beret upon his head. But his face was raised skyward and contorted in anger, while his right hand was clenched in a fist, as if railing against the gods.

"Toss it in, Watson."

Reluctantly, I did so. The instant the canvas met the heat it began to vibrate. Holmes caught my arm and pulled me back. Black, oily smoke roiled up from the fireplace, and the air itself seemed to grow harsh and heavy.

There was a loud cry, the shriek of a wounded man.

To my astonishment, the dark smoke abruptly belched forth the artist, who flew out of the fireplace with his left shirtsleeve aflame. Holmes seized a carafe of water and splashed it over him, dousing the blaze. The man fell to our carpet, moaning and writhing.

"Damn you," he hissed, looking up with a soot-smeared face. "Damn you to the Shadows! The foulest wizard in London, that is what you are, Sherlock Holmes."

My friend's face brightened with amusement at the man's verbal abuse. "Dr. Watson, I give you Mr.

Robert Vernet Smythe. Cease your whimpering, sir, and make yourself presentable. You have much to answer for."

Chapter Five

"I only did it because I was terrified," Smythe said. "What they conjured up in that place---it will kill me if it finds me!"

The artist now sat on our sofa, staring morosely into the fireplace, where the last of his magical paintings smoldered amid the ashes. While Smythe had washed his face and donned one of Holmes's old shirts, my friend had explained the astonishing process by which the painter had hidden himself from his lover and the world at large.

"His pictures were portals, Watson. Because he is made of the same magic, he could enter them at will and use them as gateways through the Shadows. As long as one existed, he could cower within it. Thus it was necessary to flush him out like the wary game that he was. I knew he would be unwilling to lock himself within the Shadows for all eternity as he bore strong feelings for Miss Simone, which he demonstrated by providing her with gifts and money."

"So he could enter and exit any of his pictures at will, no matter where they were hung?"

"Indeed, which explains how he was able to travel to Lord Whiteleigh's estate and pilfer jewels. The fact that he had not taken advantage of his extraordinary talent to do so previously---that he was content to live as a penniless artist---is in his favor. I do not believe he is a bad man, but there must be some extraordinary explanation as to why he would not simply return to his lady and claim a miraculous escape from the fire at Urian Hall."

Now, it seemed, our young painter would be forced to account for his actions. There was no need for us to attempt to restrain him or make threats. Holmes's cold silver gaze was impressive enough, and at last the dark-haired youth began to speak.

"I suppose you know of a human wizard named Etienne Lellouche?" Smythe asked.

Holmes inclined his head. "I have made his acquaintance. It was before your time, Watson, but he was a singularly dangerous man. Only a mortal wizard, but educated and skillful, and totally without moral restraint."

While these words were spoken calmly, almost carelessly, I saw something flicker on my friend's face. I would hesitate to call it fear, but it was a darkness that trembled. Momentarily, his expression became a mask of unease. Yet in a heartbeat this unease was vanquished. Clearly, there was more to this Etienne Lellouche than Holmes was willing to discuss.

"He was skillful," Smythe agreed. "And he could recognize those who have only the hint of Shadows in the blood." The painter turned to me with a self-deprecating smile. "Your friend Mr. Holmes is a Halfling. In contrast, I have only one-eighth of the Shadow ancestry, so my skills are limited to my ability to move through my own work.

Yet Etienne sought me out. He offered me a hundred pounds to come to Urian Hall and work on a commission, and he threatened me with exposure of my singular talents if I did not."

"What was your commission?" Holmes asked.

"He said only that I would soon paint a portrait of the most evil man who had ever lived. I told my darling 'famous man' in order not to frighten her, but Lellouche said *evil*." Smythe gave an exaggerated shrug. "The individuals who gathered at the manor that night were certainly not great villains, however."

"Indeed? Then who were they?" Holmes asked.

"I do not know," Smythe replied, with a quick shake of his head. Holmes cleared his throat and the young man turned, meeting his skeptical expression with pale-faced directness. "I can see you think I am lying, but on my blood, I swear I never learned the identity of the guests. Etienne called them his 'Theosophical Club,' and I assumed they were devil-worshippers or people of occult talents. But when he introduced them to me, he referred to them only as Mr. A, Mrs. B and so on. He had worked through the alphabet to F when the last member of his club arrived. I can tell you no more about them."

"You are an artist," Holmes countered, "and your living comes, in part, from your mastery of detail. Close your eyes and describe these individuals."

Smythe made a face that indicated he found the request akin to torture, but submitted without further

41

protest. "Mr. A and Mrs. B were a married couple, both of them perhaps fifty years old. She towered over him, as he was virtually a dwarf, with absurdly bowed legs. He wore an evening suit and she a black satin gown with a plunging neckline and a cascade of silk roses over the bustle. But no jewelry---neither of them had so much as a ring or a stickpin."

"Excellent," Holmes murmured. "Continue."

"They were English, of the north, based on their accents and the way the man complained about the trains. Mr. C was, I think, a local fellow, medium height and very stout, with a round head. He was quite bald, but with long ginger hairs sprouting from his ears. He had doused himself in cologne, yet beneath it I could smell a certain stench, as if he worked in blood and carcasses."

"A butcher?" I prompted.

"Perhaps. His hands were white and raw, as though he had bleached them many times to take away the stains." The artist slumped back on the sofa, folding his arms. "Mrs. D was a gypsy woman, with wild raven hair and a skirt of the most outrageous purple taffeta. She spoke little English, and seemed angry to have been summoned. At times I sensed her prattling words were those of warning. Mr. E was a younger man, tall with long dark hair, dressed in cast-off attire that did not fit him. He wore clumsy boots on his feet and heavy black spectacles over his eyes. I do not know his nationality because I never heard him speak. He did not seem to comprehend many words, and I saw Etienne guide him around, communicating in gestures. He stank like a peasant, I might add!"

"Intriguing," Holmes said. "And the last member of this club?"

"Another man, Mr. F. He was old, tall and gaunt, with the face of a skeptical scholar. He carried a Gladstone bag with him, and I guessed it was filled with books. He shifted it from one hand to the other, as if it gave him pains from its weight." The artist opened his eyes and sat back up. "That is all I can tell you, Mr. Holmes. There were no servants in the house. I was there for only a day; Etienne offered me nothing but some bread, cheese, and wine, which he might have procured at the local grocer's."

"So no party was planned?"

"I had the impression the assembly was gathered for a meeting, not a celebration." The artist scratched his chin. "I suppose you wish to know about the hall itself."

"I do."

"Etienne said he had only recently purchased it. Though built in the Georgian style the place was a ruin, the grounds run to seed and few of the rooms habitable. I made my bed on the floor in an empty room upstairs. The furnishings were covered in dust; the paper was speckled in mould and peeling from the walls. I would have guessed it was once the home of some knight or prosperous merchant, but too far removed from the town or any decent roads to be convenient."

Holmes scowled a bit, but did not ask for an enhancement of the description. "Tell us what occurred on that fateful evening," he said.

At this, the artist shook his head. "I do not know. I was ordered out of the dining room once the guests had assembled, told to go and wait in my chamber. I went upstairs and tried to distract myself. Soon there were some...*unfortunate* sounds emanating from below."

"Be precise," Holmes demanded. A thin layer of sweat had formed on the young man's brow, and he began to twist his hands together in agitation.

"Chanting. I am no adept, but I have heard wizards work. They were calling up a spirit or demon, I feel certain. And then I heard a struggle, a cry for help, followed by a dying man's wail. I think---I fear---that they were offering a sacrifice. Some type of blood magic was being performed."

Holmes's face was dark. A sharp chill passed over my own frame, for only a few weeks before we had dealt with one of the most hideous practitioners of the unholy art of blood magic. As if he sensed our discomfort, Smythe looked down at his hands.

"During all of this, I heard one exchange clearly. It was a woman---Mrs. B, I suppose---who cried out 'but where are the pages we need?' and Etienne answered her quite briskly, 'I can bring him forth without them.' Beyond that, everything was incoherent to my ears, and I tried to keep my mind at ease by drawing a sketch of a peaceful country scene. But then I heard another, even more horrible sound. It was as if a train had crashed through the building. The walls shook and an ancient brass chandelier in my room crashed to the ground, nearly impaling me. I scrambled to my feet and ran downstairs. The doors to the dining room were smashed open. I looked inside and...I am glad you are of the Shadows, Mr. Holmes, for no mortal would believe what I saw within that room."

I confess that the artist's narrative had me literally on the edge of my seat. "What was it?" I asked.

"It was *nothing*," he answered.

Chapter Six

"Nothing?"

"Perfect emptiness. Black beyond black, an infinite void that no eye could fully encompass. It hung in middle of the room like some horrible tapestry, a chasm more vast and horrible than even the Shadows could create. On the edge were flickering flames, green and hellish, and a vile stench was belching forth. I saw lightning strikes deep within it. I heard moans, screams, wild gibbering. Whatever it was, no mortal's threat could keep me in that accursed hall. I whirled, fled back to my room, and leapt to safety through my sketch. I was so fearful of being trailed that I cowered in the Shadows for two days, and when I emerged I learned the news that the hall had been destroyed and that I was presumed dead. I acknowledge my cowardice, gentlemen, but it seemed far safer to stay falsely deceased than to risk it in actuality."

Holmes touched a finger to his lips. "Did you observe what had become of the people in the room? How did they react to the appearance of the chasm?"

Again, the artist squeezed his eyes shut, working to reconstruct the image in his mind. "Mrs. B had fainted and Mr. A was bending over her. The gypsy woman was running toward a window, and Mr. F was clutching his chest. I did not see Etienne, or Mr. C. Mr. E, the man with the reek of a peasant...he was the only one not affected. He stood watching it, calm and composed, as if viewing his goats grazing on a hillside."

"And the other? The sacrifice?"

The artist flinched. "I saw a body there, a naked old man. But he had been cut into pieces."

"Did you see-"

"NO! No more! What do these questions matter? What does any of it matter, Mr. Holmes? They are all dead!"

With that, Smythe sprang from the seat, whipping his head around wildly. "I can stay no longer! Even now, I feel it."

"What do you feel?" Holmes asked.

"A pressure. A prickling. As if I am being watched by something from within that void. God help me---it knows I have seen it!"

He seized his charred beret and bolted for the door. Holmes barked at him and he froze with his hand on the knob.

"There is the matter of Miss Simone, sir. I promised to restore you to her."

"You cannot. I sent her the telegram, hoping news of my death would set her free."

"Yet you also returned to her, and your gifts speak louder than your feeble excuses," Holmes said. "You love the young lady, in a strangely honorable fashion for an artist."

Smythe bit upon his lip. His hand rattled the doorknob in agitation. "I must stay away because I love her so deeply! I do not want her cursed by this thing."

"Then take her to the Shadows."

Smythe's jaw fell, his eyes bulged. "You cannot be serious, Mr. Holmes! To let a mortal know of the Shadows---it would kill her!"

Holmes gestured toward where I sat. "Watson knows of the Shadows and he seems hale enough. And need I remind you that our very existence proves that mortals have mingled with the Shadows from time immemorial? At least give her the choice."

The artist shuddered, but slowly raised a hand as if taking an oath. "I will, I promise. But do not expect to see me again. I will take my Venus and live in the Shadows forever rather than walk in a world where that hideous *thing* has been released!"

With that declaration, he departed, slamming our door with some force. I shook my head. "Holmes, what is this about? Surely you can make it clear to me."

My friend rose and, as was his custom, began to pace. "Our young artist has, it appears, witnessed the summoning of a wraith."

"A wraith is a ghost, is it not?"

"To be more precise, a wraith is a spirit freed from Hell. It is a formless mass of energy, a soul escaped from the pit. But unlike a ghost, which can reassume the shape it bore in life, a wraith remains incorporeal." Holmes waved a hand. "Our young friend was confused on one point---producing demons requires a different set of enchantments, as you well know."

I thought back to that day in Prague, when Doctor Dee, Holmes's own tutor in magic, had summoned Mephistopheles within the confines of the circle drawn by the legendary Faust. It was not a feat I would wish to witness again. Holmes inclined his head, acknowledging the memory.

"Any conjurer willing to accept the damnation of blood magic can bring forth a wraith. This act does not require a circle. Releasing a soul from Hades is a spectacular effect, but appallingly easy to achieve."

"And dangerous!" I said. "Surely the wraith burned down Urian Hall."

Holmes retrieved his pipe. He struck a match, staring into the flame. "No, I do not believe the wraith had the power to destroy the hall immediately upon its summoning. More likely, one of the terrified witnesses overturned a candle or a lamp. The old house, a perfect firetrap based on our artist's description, did the rest."

"Either way, we have no witnesses who can tell us who—or should I say what?—was brought forth."

"You err, I fear, on the side of incomplete data," Holmes corrected. "I went to Reading yesterday, before I began collecting the paintings, and one of my friends on the local constabulary showed me photographs they had made of the bodies. The victims were horribly charred and deformed, but one thing was clear—there were only seven corpses, and one was deliberately cut apart before the fire touched him. Therefore one of the company escaped, beyond our artist."

I felt a thrill of excitement, the way I always did at the start of an adventure. "Which one?"

Holmes leaned against the mantel. "Two of the corpses were, even in their horrific state, delicate enough to be classified as female, which takes Mrs. B and Mrs. D off the list. Another retained significant girth, and therefore was more likely to have been the local butcher, Mr. C, while a fourth was extremely short with bowed legs. Here we have Mr. A. The last two bodies were probably over six feet in height, with no distinguishing features to help in identification. Thus we have three possibilities for the survivor: the elderly scholar, Etienne the conjurer, or the mysterious 'peasant'."

I pondered this for a moment. It seemed impossible; the missing man could be one of three, and two of them were completely unknown to us except for vague depictions.

"What about the wraith?" I asked. "Is there any way to know whose soul has escaped from the pit?"

"Of all the millions of human souls in Hell, you think I can deduce which one was called forth?" Holmes's lips came together in an expression all his own: not a grimace, but an ironic acknowledgement. "I thank you for the compliment, Watson, and I will strive to merit it. We know that Etienne Lellouche spoke of this wraith as 'the most evil man who ever lived'---ah, so half the deceased population is eliminated! But who could this infamous gentleman be?"

A dozen names popped into my head, figures from history and from more recent news. I thought of killers, traitors, and villains of all descriptions. But one name rang the loudest. I looked to Holmes with some trepidation.

"Moriarty?" I asked.

Chapter Seven

Holmes considered my suggestion. After a moment, he shook his head.

"The weight of logic is against it being Moriarty," he said, "if for no other reason than, had the Napoleon of Crime risen from the abyss, I would have been done to death by now. I can still see his eyes staring up at me, their hateful gaze boring into me even as he fell amid the spray and the rocks of the Reichenbach Falls. No, it is not my old rival."

"Then we shall never know the wraith's identity."

Holmes settled back into his chair, shaking his head at me. "Let us approach this as an intellectual problem. We must dig deeper and worker harder! Imagine, Watson, if you had just fled a region of eternal torture and suffering---what would be your first desire?"

I gave his question serious consideration. "I suppose it would be to know pleasure. To eat and drink again, to talk and laugh with friends, perhaps to sample the delights of female companionship."

"In other words, you would wish to return to the life you had led before your damnation."

"Of course. But to do so I would need a body."

"Precisely my point. As an incorporeal wraith, this wicked one can know no pleasure. He must find a body to possess, and he must do it quickly or risk dissipating into the ether, becoming true *nothingness* for all eternity. But he will be weak from his long confinement, and his ability to possess and control a living body will be strained---even a small struggle would drive him from an unwilling host."

"So what will he do?"

"To become his own man, he must reanimate a corpse. He will use dead flesh to return to life."

I grimaced as another very unpleasant memory played out in my mind. "A zombie."

Holmes scowled. "No, he will not be a zombie, for a zombie is a mindless hunk of tissue. He will become indistinguishable from the lot of humanity, as in essence he will be an old soul wearing new skin."

"And he can do this alone?" I asked, fighting a shudder of revulsion. I was grateful when Holmes shook his head.

"To live again he will need a spellbook and a helper to speak the words he can not utter. He requires an accomplice to cast that spell that will bind his soul to a body and give him renewed mortality." Holmes tapped the tips of his fingers together. "One wonders if Lellouche planned for more than a blood sacrifice to raise the wraith. Perhaps he had more sinister plans for one of his purported guests." Holmes nodded thoughtfully. "I believe our friend Smythe had a very narrow escape. If Lellouche could have sent the wraith into a mortal possessed of Shadowblood to any degree, the wraith would have become very powerful indeed."

"But wait," I said, "would any wraith know that it could be reborn in a dead body? You seem to be describing the plans of a wraith who understands magic."

Holmes smiled archly. "Watson, you scintillate tonight. You have the right of it. An evil emperor, a tyrant, a murderer might rise from Hell, but would be at a loss as to how to find and control either the living or the dead. An undead wizard, however, would possess the knowledge to seek an earthly form. And while we have no certainty of his motivations, it seems likely that a wizard like Etienne Lellouche would seek to raise another of his order. Thus, you see, our list of suspects narrows."

"To how many?" I asked.

"Several thousand," he answered airily, "that I am aware of."

With that pronouncement, my friend lapsed into silence. I knew the signs and felt it best not to interrupt his meditations. A guest to our rooms would have assumed Holmes asleep, as still as he was. Only the rapid movements of his eyes beneath closed lids gave a clue to the intensity of his thoughts. I picked up a newspaper, seeking to divert myself. A small article caught my attention. I considered Holmes, wondering if I dared to speak.

"One moment, Watson. I have just a few further questions to put to you before you tell me the shocking news you have just read in the *Times*."

His eyes were still shuttered. "Holmes, how did you know that I was about to alert you? Once you promised to never use your Shadow powers on me--- have you forgotten than pledge?"

"Hardly. I am not deaf," he said, with an edge of exasperation, "thus your sudden gasp of breath, rustle of newsprint, and unsubtle clearing of the throat clearly announced your intentions. But answer an inquiry before you do so: who was the greatest bandit who ever lived?"

I was utterly baffled by this sudden twist of subject. "Why, that would be Robin Hood."

"And the noblest king?"

I shrugged. "Arthur, naturally."

"Hmmm...and the greatest military commander?"

"The Duke of Wellington. But what is your point?"

He opened his eyes. "My point, Doctor, is that mankind is by nature a patriotic species. When asked to name superlatives, there is an excellent chance that he will choose individuals of his own race and country. You could as easily have named Jesse James or Rob Roy for your bandit, but you thought immediately of Robin Hood. Was Charlemagne not a noble king? Louis IX of France and Stephen I of Hungary are both venerated as saints, yet I wager their names never crossed your mind. And will you truly elevate Wellington over Caesar? That is rather unsporting!"

"An intriguing observation, but I fail to see how this is helpful."

"Etienne Lellouche was a wizard. He announced his intention to raise the most evil man who ever lived. Does it not stand to reason that such a man as Lellouche would give this unsavory endorsement to a fellow Gaul?"

"So we are looking for a French wizard!"

"It is possible. More than that, it is probable." Holmes leapt from the chair and grabbed a volume from the index. "One name rises to the top. Tell me, Watson, have you ever heard of Gilles de Rais?"

I confessed my ignorance. Holmes placed the book on his table and motioned me to his side. He pointed down at an illustration of a devil chatting amiably with a man in a long robe. The devil's companion had the rough face and close cropped hair of a soldier, with fierce whiskers on his chin. In one hand he held a long knife, and in the other the bloody, severed head of a child.

"Born circa 1405, the heir of a noble name," Holmes said. "He fought with Joan of Arc and was considered a pious man, one who gave freely to the construction of chapels and cathedrals. He retired to his castle at Machecoul in 1432, and soon began to waste his family's fortune on excessive revels and renovations. His relatives feared that his excesses would bankrupt the clan, but his celebrations masked a far greater sin."

Holmes's lean finger touched the broken body of the youth at the man's feet.

"Gilles de Rais had become a devil-worshipper, a conjurer, and a sodomite. Many boys were sacrificed in his black rituals, but only after he had profaned their bodies in unspeakable acts. He lured them to his castle with promises of wealth and promotion. He even bought them from their families, insisting he would educate them and make them knights. Soon the small villages all around were depleted of their sons, and the poor people began to cry for justice. At last, the Bishop of Nantes made an inquiry, and in 1440 Gilles de Rais was arrested and indicted on numerous counts of murder. But that was only a fraction of the terror he had inflicted. The priests and knights who came into his castle found elaborate torture chambers and altars to Lucifer. Gilles de Rais broke under threat of the same tortures he had inflicted on his victims, and gave details of behaviors that sent hardened soldiers fleeing from his cell. On October 26, 1440, he was hanged and his body burned."

"But if he was truly such a powerful sorcerer, how was he ever captured?" I asked. "I mean no offense by the comparison, but I cannot imagine that you would allow yourself to be meekly taken by any force that sought to do you harm."

"I thank you for your allowances, Watson. There are two answers to your most intelligent question. The traditional one is that Satan, the father of lies, abandoned his follower just as he deludes all who sacrifice to him, and gave his devotee over to death so that he might harvest a damned soul. The other, however, involves a brave female servant, who glimpsed a certain truth---that Gilles de Rais owned a spellbook bound in human skin. Without this book, the conjurer was powerless, for he was a mortal wizard. On the evening that the knights and priests advanced on his castle, Gilles de Rais hurried to his lair to take the book and unleash spells that would blast his enemies to dust, only to find that the book had been stolen from him."

I barely resisted the urge to clap at the heroics Holmes described. "And what became of his book?"

"It was burned on the pyre along with its owner."

"Then there is nothing to fear! If Gilles de Rais's spells have been destroyed..."

My words trailed away. Holmes was favoring me with a look of weary amusement. I understood even before he spoke.

"There are more spellbooks."

"Many more, my dear Watson. My tutor Doctor Dee owns over a thousand. And such a book will be the one object the wraith will covet above all else, because within it will rest the magic that he needs to bring himself fully back to life. And once that happens..."

58

His eyes dropped back to the page, to the image of the slaughtered child. Horror wrapped around my throat like skeletal hands.

"Why Gilles de Rais?" I asked. "What could Etienne Lellouche have hoped to learn from him?"

"We must tread carefully, Watson, for we are working on substantial presumptions, but even these could give way to solid facts that might completely alter the nature of this case. I would prefer to work with more data." Holmes tapped the book with urgency. "I must learn more."

"You had hoped to avoid the Shadows," I noted. Holmes's response was wry smile.

"Indeed....but you were about to tell me something," Holmes whispered.

"Yes, it is about Inspector Gregson."

Holmes snorted. "What foolish pronouncement has he made this time?"

"Holmes, his brother is dead."

Chapter Eight

The interment was in the Brookwood cemetery, outside of London, and we reached the grounds just as the service for Thomas Gregson was concluding. It distressed me to see that the party was so small in number: only a young nonconformist priest, Inspector Gregson, Inspector Lestrade, and a woman swathed in black were in attendance. We paused beside some tombs as the last prayer was being spoken. The churchman whispered a few words and hurried away, a dark grimace on his face, as if he had found his job distasteful. The trio at the tomb consulted among themselves. Lestrade offered his arm to the lady and together they moved toward us, leaving Gregson staring into the grave. Holmes nodded to me and we stepped into the narrow lane to meet the departing couple.

"Mr. Holmes, Dr. Watson," Lestrade greeted us. "You're too late, I fear."

"It was only brought to my attention a short time ago," Holmes allowed. "It is a great tragedy for our friend."

Lestrade quickly introduced the lady as Mrs. Gregson. She was a plain woman in appearance, but with an open face and a gentle gaze that no doubt was comforting to a man in her spouse's hard line of work.

"My husband is convinced that his brother was murdered, despite all evidence to the contrary. Mr. Holmes, I have read of your great powers. Please, if you will, do help my darling to understand what has happened. I fear that his mind has been nearly unhinged by this."

"I will do all that I can," Holmes promised.

Lestrade indicated that they were returning to London immediately, and with a quick tip of his hat, they disappeared amidst the monuments. Holmes asked me to wait. He walked to Gregson and put a hand on his shoulder. I do not know what words my friend offered, but after a few moments Gregson nodded and agreed to accompany us. The mortuary train had just departed, but the attendant assured us another one would be along soon. Holmes led us to the small café inside the meager station, ordering coffee and biscuits for us while we waited.

I have always lacked Holmes's ability to know a person's occupation or state of mind from his garb, but even a novice like myself could tell that Gregson had not slept in days. His eyes were red, the flesh beneath them raw and bruised. His shaving was haphazard, with a half-dozen cuts to his chin and one plane of his face missed entirely and covered in stubble. Bereavement and mourning were familiar to me in my work as a physician, but this was something more.

"Will you accept my case?" the inspector said, after a long introspection of the black fluid in his cup. "I have fought the thing with no results, and it is time that I acknowledge it must be laid at the feet of a master, not carried forward by an apprentice."

Holmes nodded. For all his mocking of the regular police detectives, he liked them as individuals, the way a woman might carry a fondness for hapless lovers. When he spoke, his voice was kind.

"Would you not prefer to wait until tomorrow morning, when you have rested and put this grim day behind you?"

Gregson shook his head. "I must tell you now, if you will listen."

Holmes opened his silver case and fished out a cigarette. Gregson accepted Holmes's offer, nodding over the flare of the match as Holmes lit the cigarette for him. "I will do all that I can for you," Holmes said. "Tell me what happened to your brother."

Gregson's eyes narrowed, and his words hissed through his teeth. "He was murdered, Mr. Holmes. Killed in cold blood. But how in God's name can I prove it when half a dozen witnesses saw my brother throw himself from Tower Bridge?" The inspector shuddered, but after a moment he exhaled, as if the tobacco had calmed him. "I suppose I should do as we tell our witnesses, and start at the beginning."

"As we already know the sad conclusion, it would be preferable," Holmes coaxed.

Gregson drew a deep breath. "Thomas was my only brother, younger than me by two years. We were great companions in boyhood, always tussling and tumbling, getting into mischief together until our parents despaired of us. We were determined that we should join some regiment, as we were both excellent marksmen--- our small home was covered with trophies from our hunts. But when Thomas turned fifteen, he developed an ocular disease. He was left nearly blind and forced to wear the most tremendous spectacles imaginable. He was so humiliated by his infirmity that his entire personality changed. He became reclusive and scholarly.

"Our family was not wealthy; there was only enough money to send one of us to the university. I insisted that Thomas have it, thinking that he would rise to be a college don. Instead, he became an antiquarian, a specialist in ancient documents and manuscripts. He worked for a time in the Bodleian Library of Oxford, then, five years ago, he moved to London and set up a small shop in Holywell Street."

"Did your brother have a family?" Holmes asked.

"No. His vision had continued to decline. He once described it to me as looking through a tiny tube, unable to see anything to the side. He was able to view what was before him only with the most potent of lens. I used to argue with him that plenty of blind men met and married good ladies, but he preferred his quiet life. I think he grew to love his books and papers more than any normal man could love a woman. I finally accepted that my brother would be a queer old bachelor, like a character out of one of Mr. Dickens's novels, and I was grateful that he was happy with his work and his strange collections. Because of our respective careers, we visited rather infrequently. Therefore I was shocked when he was escorted into my office at Scotland Yard just over a week ago, in a state of extreme terror.

"'Good heavens, Thomas, what's come over you?' I asked, for I had never seen him in such a state. My brother was not a hale and hearty fellow, but he was no coward. Once he had managed to thrash a local ruffian who had tried to make off with some trinket from his shop---though, in all fairness, he did more damage to his store than to the man. 'You look as if you have seen a ghost,' I said.

"'Not a ghost, but the devil! I believe it was the devil himself who came to my store this morning!'

"A strong dose of brandy settled his nerves enough that he could tell me his story. It seemed that a customer had arrived just as he opened his door. The man was tall, clad in a great black cape and high hat, with very dark spectacles over his eyes and his long hair pulled into a strange braid, like a Chinaman might wear. He introduced himself as Count Kirov, a Russian nobleman and intimate of the Czar, and hinted that he was on a collecting expedition for that worthy.

"'You will excuse my assistant,' he said, drawing something from inside his cloak, 'but he has a horror of the English dampness and prefers not to expose himself to its rigors.'"

"And then, as if it were the most natural thing in the world, he settled a doll onto the chair beside him."

I nearly dropped the delicate china cup from which I had been sipping my coffee. "A doll?"

Gregson drew a trembling hand over his face. "God forgive me, but when my brother told me this, I laughed in his face. Surely the client was some witless eccentric, a candidate for Bedlam. But my brother reached across the table and seized my wrist in a grip as cold as death, and threatened to never speak to me again if I gave so much as another chuckle. It was that grip, and the look that his immense spectacles only amplified, that told me my poor sibling was nearly mad with terror."

Holmes frowned. I suspected he found this development as bizarre and inexplicable as Gregson had, when it occurred. "How did he describe the figure?"

"It was a sailor doll, he said, the image of a male child in blue pantaloons and a red-striped shirt, the head crafted of porcelain and the limbs of cloth. The entire doll was no more than three feet tall. The Count propped it in a chair and took some pains with it, as if it were a real boy he sought to make comfortable. Then he turned back to my brother and began to make inquiries."

Holmes lifted a hand. "One moment. Did your brother say if this Count Kirov presented any credentials?"

Gregson shook his head. "I asked Thomas the same thing, at just this juncture. He said no, but that did not surprise him. He often had clients who---for some reason---prefer to mask their identity, many of them in a very clumsy and theatrical fashion."

Holmes nodded. "A practice I am also familiar with. Watson, you no doubt recall the Count Von Kramm?"

"I do. He was, in actuality, the King of Bohemia."

"I doubt this man was as equally distinguished," Gregson demurred, "but my brother chose not to challenge him. Indeed, he said it required all his concentration and nerve to follow the Count's questions, for his eyes, poor as they were, were drawn to the inanimate figure in the chair beside his client. The Count asked to view a number of ancient documents, and as he spoke my brother noticed another curious aspect to this client. His English was broken and heavily accented, sometimes with French inflections. But often it seemed that his words did not match the workings of his lips. It was, Thomas said, as if the figure beside him was speaking and casting his voice to the other, like a ventriloquist on a music hall stage; only this time, the puppet was manipulating the master. In the end, the Russian chose not to purchase any of the manuscripts he had viewed, but promised he would return later. He gathered up the doll and tucked it away inside his cape, rising and making as if to exit with absurd pleasantries.

"'And then,' Thomas said, 'the Count did the most horrible thing. He lifted his spectacles and---my God!---he looked at me. Looked at me so strangely, with those horrible, horrible eyes!'

"My brother was shaking so violently he nearly fell from his chair. I quizzed him further, but he admitted there had been no threat, no obvious warning of danger. The man had stolen nothing, yet Thomas was so terrorized by the strange doll and that brief second of gazing into the Count's eyes that he was reduced to jelly. He had locked up his store and was now begging my protection.

"Mr. Holmes, I am ashamed of what I did next. I dismissed my brother's fears as some type of breakdown from overwork. I coddled him the way one would a hysterical woman, thinking that with a few days' rest he would come to his senses and we would have a merry laugh over the matter. I even tried to persuade him to return to his business, warning him that he would lose a significant commission if he were not there. But he refused, saying that he had lost the only thing that could protect him from evil. And so I took him to my home, where he locked himself a room and it was all my wife and I could do to get him to come down and take meals with us."

"Wait! Did your brother say what it was that he had lost?" Holmes asked.

Gregson scowled in annoyance at my friend's interruption. "No. I asked him, half in jest, if he had acquired a gun or a medieval mace, but he only moaned and would speak no more of it. I let the matter drop, as he seemed insensible."

Holmes nodded. "Please continue."

"Half a week passed in this manner. But on Sunday, Thomas abruptly came down to breakfast and apologized for his strange behavior. He said he could not imagine what it was that had possessed him. He vowed to return to his home immediately, but I insisted that we spend the morning together. My wife went off to church while Thomas and I took a rather aimless stroll around the metropolis. By noon we found ourselves at the Tower. We stayed almost an hour and Thomas amused me with stories of the dark and bloody deeds done there, drawing on the many documents that had passed through his store. He insisted that we walk across Tower Bridge for a better view of the edifice."

Gregson hesitated, drawing a deep breath. I could sense the struggle it required for him to compose his words with care and without emotion. If a staunch police inspector was so affected, the horror of the event must have been nearly unbearable.

"We were standing at the railing, admiring the great relic. I thought I heard a voice call my name. I looked around, but saw no one among the passing pedestrians who seemed to be signaling to me or whom I recognized. I shrugged and turned back to my brother, only to witness a transformation in him. His face had gone ashen, and behind his spectacles his eyes were as wild as those of a panicked horse. He gave an inarticulate screech and began waving his arms wildly. His coat flapped all about him. I was frozen to the spot. I thought he was having some type of seizure. Then he screamed the words that I will take to my grave:

"'Those eyes! Those horrible eyes!'

"And with that my poor brother threw himself backward over the railing and plunged to his death in the black water of the Thames."

Chapter Nine

Gregson twisted his hands together, his fingers pressed so roughly I felt sure they would break from the intensity of his checked emotion. "I was climbing up to go after him, but two stout lads grabbed me and held me back. I could do him no good. It took time to find his body. I suppose I was lucky even to be able to bury him."

My friend had been staring at the ceiling throughout this recitation. His gaze returned to Gregson, and when he spoke it was with the studied gentleness that I had so often heard him use on his more fragile clients.

"I know this will be difficult, Inspector, but there are some more specific questions I must put to you."

"Of course," Gregson whispered.

"You say your brother threw himself from the bridge *backwards*?"

"Yes. It sounds incredible, but in my memory he seems to be lifted up, as if invisible hands had seized his lapels. There was an instant---a heartbeat, no more---that he shook in midair. Then he was gone. My last vision of him was a flash of his heels as he toppled over the edge."

Holmes frowned. "And the voice that called to you---you did not recognize it?"

"No. In fact...I now think it was directed at my brother. It was but one word: 'Gregson.'"

"And he turned as well at the call?"

"I believe that he did."

"No person on the bridge stood out to you in any way?"

Gregson shook his head. "It was a typical Sunday crowd. I saw nothing memorable."

I could sense that Holmes was suppressing a sigh of impatience. "Tell me of the robbery at your brother's shop."

The Inspector jerked so sharply he nearly overturned his coffee. "You are a wizard indeed, Mr. Holmes! Yes, when I went to his property that evening, I found that the lock on the rear door had been broken. A rug was kicked aside, but I could find no footprints or any trace of a clue." Gregson raked one hand through his hair. "Nor was there anything taken, in either his shop or his dwelling, which was on the floor above."

"You are certain?"

Gregson seemed poised to assent, but at the last second deflated, slumping back in his chair. "No, Mr. Holmes, I am not. My brother, you see, never kept records. It was all in here, he used to tell me." Gregson tapped his own skull with a sad smile. "His privacy was so sacred to him that he would never employ a clerk or even a housekeeper. I have no way of knowing if anything is missing, for I do not know what was there! A few items---a watch, a ruby stickpin, and a pair of gold doubloons---were on his dresser, unmolested. Surely a thief would have snatched those things, which could easily have been converted to cash."

Holmes shook his head. "From what you have told me, Inspector, your brother possessed far more valuable articles. Do I have your permission to inspect his residence?"

In reply, Gregson pulled out a brass key and placed it in Holmes's hand, explaining that he had called in a man to repair the lock, but otherwise his brother's home and shop remained as they had been when Thomas abandoned them. "I touched very little, and removed nothing except a photograph of our parents, which I later placed in his coffin."

Holmes rose. "I am deeply sorry for you loss, Inspector. I will do all that I can."

"So you think he was murdered? My brother's mind had never been clouded before, and I cannot accept that he simply went mad." Gregson's drawn face was one of the most pathetic things I had ever beheld. "Do you agree with me, that Thomas was somehow driven to this, *assassinated* into some manner?"

"I believe that his case bears further inquiry," Holmes said. "But you must get some rest. And from the familiar sounds outside this place, it is clear that our train has arrived. Let us speak of happier things as we return home."

We bid the inspector farewell at the London station. Holmes sent me on to Baker Street, while he took time to send some telegrams. As usual, he did not reveal their contents. I watched the darkening sky with sinking spirits, thinking of my own poor brother. Holmes had once divined his entire sad history from a reading of the watch that that I had inherited from him. I found myself hoping that Holmes could provide Gregson with more comfort than I had found from his *tour de force* of deduction.

Holmes returned just as Mrs. Hudson was placing a meal before us. He halted her as she started to lower the platter of roast woodcock to the table.

"Mrs. Hudson, could I beg your assistance? I have a small investigation that only you can undertake."

For an instant I thought she would dump our dinner in his lap. Our good landlady's face registered shock, surprise, and more than a full measure of suspicion.

"Now, Mr. Holmes, I'm not as young as I used to be. I'm not sure that my knees will take crawling around this room again, with bullets crashing all about the place."

My friend's smile was genuine. "I promise you, Mrs. Hudson, this will not be dangerous. I merely need you to find the shop where a certain doll was sold."

"A doll?"

Holmes gave her an exact description of the plaything that had accompanied the mysterious Russian. "You will go to all the fashionable toy shops, looking for this item. You will accept no substitutes, for this is the very thing that your beloved granddaughter has demanded for her birthday. If you find it, you will purchase it and bring it directly to me." He pulled a small velvet pouch from his pocket, emptying a handful of coins into her shaking palm. "That should be sufficient to cover your costs, including the doll. Will you help me?"

"Yes, but what will you do for dinner tomorrow?"

"I am sure we can survive on our own. Thank you, Mrs. Hudson. That will be all."

"But what is the meaning of the doll?" I asked, after our landlady had departed. "I assumed the Russian was insane."

"Watson, surely by now you see that nothing is pointless. There is no room for ordinary madness in the Shadows. Do finish your meal, as we must leave immediately."

I had barely time to consume three bites before Holmes was ordering me into my coat and dragging me down the stairs. Our destination was Thomas Gregson's odd little shop in Holywell Street, which we reached just as the streetlamps were being lit. A mourning wreath hung on the door, along with a sign indicating the shop was closed until further notice. I wondered what the inspector would do with the treasures his sibling had left behind. I somehow communicated my thoughts to Holmes through unconscious actions or expressions, and he answered them in that unnerving manner that brought him such great amusement.

"In a few days, a private dealer will make an astonishing offer for the entire inventory of this store. Inspector Gregson will be inclined to take it, as he knows nothing of the real value of his late brother's holdings."

I immediately grasped my friend's meaning. "And you will be that dealer, in disguise?"

Holmes gave a thin smile. "I would not push my luck so far with Gregson, who has a better eye than Lestrade or Jones, whom I have tricked in the past. And considering his loss, it would be cruel to play the imposter with him. I will send one of my many associates."

"So you do plan to acquire this shop's materials. Why?"

Holmes slipped the key into the lock. "Because I suspect that not all of the papers and manuscripts within this shop are mere historical curiosities. Most would be better served by being placed in a museum or archives, for the use of dedicated researchers. But some, quite frankly, must be confined."

He pushed into the shop and turned up the lights. The store was small; a single room crowded with books, papers, and framed documents. Some volumes were stacked high in columns, which in turn were half-collapsed, giving the place the appearance of an ancient ruin, a Pompeii or Roman forum made not of marble, but of paper. A single large table sat at the rear, with well-worn chairs for the shopkeeper and clients. Holmes pointed to a substantial ledger, opening it carefully and drawing a finger down the names and descriptions of the transactions.

"It seems Thomas Gregson kept excellent records of what he sold, and to whom, but there appears to be no corresponding catalog of what he owned."

"Then how can we know what is missing, if anything?"

Holmes considered the musty layers of the cluttered room. "It will require a great deal of patience and a very precise instrument."

He pulled his magnifying glass from his pocket. With an apology, he asked me to investigate the late gentleman's abode, which was to the rear and in the flat above the store. I was flattered at his trust, but I suspected my own search would be in vain. What could I find that Thomas's own brother had missed? Still, I made my way into the private areas, poking my head into every nook and cranny of the tiny kitchen, the bare bathroom, and a bedroom that was so spartan it might have housed a monk or a prisoner. There was nothing to give a clue as to Thomas Gregson's personality: not so much as a print from a sporting journal tacked to the wall, or a ticket stub from a favorite play tucked into the frame of a mirror. A wardrobe held two suits of the most conventional type, and the bed linens, curtains, and other furnishings were cheap and nondescript. I opened every drawer, finding nothing more intriguing than socks in need of darning and a few shirt collars. It was only when I gave one drawer an extra shove (brought on, no doubt, by my growing frustration with my task) that I heard a tiny plinking sound, as if something had fallen to the floor beneath the chest. I knelt and squinted into the dust. There I saw a bronze artifact the size of a lady's pendant. I fished it out, taking it to the gas lamp for better illumination.

It was a strange item, an ornament shaped roughly like a human hand with an outward turned palm. The fingers of the outline were traced in bronze, and within the hand was a delicate filigree of metalwork that, the more I considered it, seemed to spell out a message in the hieroglyphs of ancient Egypt. At the very center of the palm was a strange jewel, an opal inset with an amethyst, which in turn was inset with a tiny pinpoint of ebony. The effect was of an artificial eye, staring out from the middle of the hand. There was a small loop of metal at the top of the wrist; perhaps the token was usually worn on a chain or string. The smoothness on the back of the device assured me that it had at some time been pressed to human skin.

Intrigued with my find, I returned to the shop. Holmes was standing at the desk, glaring down at a huge bound volume. He snapped his head around, addressing me before I could alert him to my discovery.

"This was a fool's errand, Watson. While I have found Thomas Gregson's ingenious hiding place, I am no closer to knowing what item has been stolen."

I gestured to the large book. "What is it?"

"A type of safe, you might say. Clearly, our friend had an idea that a certain document was valuable, but lacking any type of vault he devised an ingenious method to keep it secure, one which I credit myself for anticipating." Holmes moved to a shelf, tapping four other large editions. "I imagined myself in a similar situation, wishing to have a document handy, but not exposed. Where in a store such as this might I hide it, in plain sight as it were? The answer was obvious: I would conceal it inside another, virtually worthless book. I could pull this book down and remove the valuable document whenever I wished. If you will use my lens, Watson, you will observe that the dust has been recently disturbed in five separate places. The inspector told us his brother exhibited several articles to his clients---we can trace them through the newly cleaned lines on the shelf. Four of these have proved to be items of no particular interest: a genealogy of Hungarian monarchs, a twelfth-century bestiary, a rather poorly illustrated copy of Foxe's *Book of Martyrs*, and a schoolboy's edition of Caesar's *Commentaries*. None of those seems relevant to our inquiry. But this final one---observe."

Holmes drew me back to the table and opened the immense volume. The pages had been carefully cut and removed, forming a kind of chamber inside the book.

"But what has been taken?" I asked.

"That is the problem. I had hoped some impression might remain, some scrap of paper or spill of ink. But our thief has been careful to remove his spoils completely, and has cleaned the inside of this remarkable container, leaving not even dust to tell a tale. Our object may be this size—or smaller. It may be a book, a document, or an artefact. Without any kind of record, and the previous owner deceased, there is simply no way to know what his unusual client was after. We may, I think, work on the safe hypothesis that the Russian was the one who broke the latch and removed an article from this hiding place."

It did seem an end to our investigation. I could tell from the look on Holmes's face that he took it as a personal affront to be so stymied. "Do you think it was magical?" I asked.

He expanded his hand over the vacant space between the incised pages. "I find it rather unlikely that any thieves would go to such trouble to steal something that was not uniquely valuable. After all, I can point to at least twenty other items in this store that, at auction, might fetch a hundred pounds or more. Whatever was in this container was very precious, but whether to the world of Sun or Shadow I cannot with certainty say."

His extended hand brought me back to the object in my own. I held it out to him, stating where I had found it.

The effect on Holmes was remarkable. His eyes widened and he breathed sharply, as if stabbed by some invisible blade. I tried to make him take it, but instead he insisted that I hold it out, allowing him to study it with the glass.

"What is it?" I asked.

"A hamsa, Watson," he replied. "It is also called 'the hand of Mary' in Christian tradition, 'the hand of Fatima' by our Muslim brethren, and 'the hand of Miriam' by the Jews. It is a powerful talisman or charm, protecting the wearer..."

His words trailed away. He straightened, sniffing the air.

"Protecting the wearer from what, Holmes?"

"The evil eye." Holmes spoke softly, quoting Gregson. "Those eyes...those horrible eyes."

Fascinated, I was anxious for him to continue, to make the connections that I had not yet established. But even as I arranged the words of my next question, he whirled around, like a dog that hears some warning sound beyond the safe walls of his master's study and bares his teeth to meet the threat.

"Watson!" he yelled, seizing me by the shoulders and jerking me from my feet, "Get down! Now!"

Chapter Ten

I heard the sharp sound of breaking glass and then, with not a second in between, felt an explosion of heat all around me. I drew myself into a ball, my hands over my head, but somehow I was not incinerated. A moment later, I heard the whoosh and roar of fire leaping out, enveloping the kindling of the store with ferocious fury. I twisted and blinked. An inferno was spreading all around us.

Holmes was holding out one arm, his hand spread wide. An invisible shield had formed, keeping the sudden crackling and popping of the firestorm at bay. Already the flames were devouring the columns of books, leaping like mad sprites from shelf to shelf, and scaling the ceiling to drop down a curtain of destruction.

And only then did I realize that the fire was not red or orange, but a vivid, searing shade of green.

"Come!" Holmes yelled, grabbing me by my collar. His wall around us held, and we dove through the door into the kitchen. The flames shot behind us and we were spit through the rear portal like two projectiles from a circus cannon. I rolled and spun until I slammed against a stone wall. Half dazed, I saw Holmes rising to his feet, confronting the blaze behind us. The fire moved faster than any I had ever seen, twisting and writhing, a living creature made of flames. As I watched, it crawled up the walls and dove back inside, blasting through the window in the rear of Thomas Gregson's small flat like an immense serpent lunging at prey. A stream of green fire shot from the chimney then plunged back down, threading its way through the roof.

To my further astonishment, the flames made no attempt to move to the houses that pressed against the shop on either side. Only the small store and the rooms above were in any danger.

"What is that?" I cried.

"Hellfire," Holmes said, with almost despicable calmness. "I think it is safe to say that whatever was stolen from Thomas Gregson was magical, as our opponents have the ability to use the fuel of Hades to cover their traces."

Holmes motioned for me to follow, but when he turned and began to run he was far too fleet for me to stay at his side. I could only limp along, and once he made two turns, I was left behind and lost in a warren of streets. I lacked Holmes's encyclopedic knowledge of London, and as crowds began to form, with people racing out of their dwellings and shouting for assistance, I soon found myself drowning in a sea of bodies. Unable to chart my own course, I finally grabbed a lamppost and clung to it, watching as citizens ran out with buckets and, in a matter of minutes, a fire truck came clattering along, bell clanging and horses frothing.

"It is no use. He was far too fast."

I turned to find Holmes at my side. With a quick apology for leaving me, he nodded toward the engulfed building. It burned with the strange green color, and the atmosphere all around us reeked of sulfur. Many of the brave fellows who had raced in to help fight the blaze were now being driven back, handkerchiefs pressed to their faces.

"Can they extinguish this fire?" I asked.

"No," Holmes said. "Hellfire only dies when it has consumed what it was tasked for. Mr. Gregson's building will be rendered to ashes in a matter of minutes, along with any clues that might have remained within."

"They know you are on their trail."

Holmes shrugged. I found I could not be so blasé about our narrow escape. It was one thing to be chased by villains with guns and knives, quite another to nearly be immolated by the fires of Hades. Holmes gave my shoulder a pat.

"Or, it is simply possible that our felon now felt confident enough to destroy any remaining evidence." Holmes offered an odd smile. "If so, we were merely at the wrong place at the wrong time."

I worked to suppress a shudder. Holmes considered me with cold dispassion.

"It is a pity the hamsa is gone."

For a moment I failed to take his meaning. Then I looked down at my hand, which was still clenched in a fist. Slowly, almost fearfully, I opened my fingers.

The charm still rested in my palm. I had squeezed it so tightly that an impression of it had formed on my flesh. The delicate filigree was bent in places, but otherwise unharmed. Holmes gave a deep sigh of relief.

"Forgive me for doubting you, Watson. And believe me when I say that you have never held a more important object than this. Guard it with your life and it will guard yours." We had reached an open avenue, and Holmes raised an arm to signal a cab.

"I will be grateful to return to Baker Street," I confessed. Holmes leapt up easily, but shocked me by giving the driver an address that I knew to be within Whitechapel.

"*The Quill and Scroll*? But that is..."

Holmes considered my broken words as the conveyance began to roll. "Our access to the Library of the Arcane and the Lady Hypatia. It is essential that I consult with her without delay."

"Why?"

"Because of that unique charm you now carry in your hand. I would advise you to transfer it to the breast pocket of your jacket, Watson. It will be safer there until we can procure a chain for you, so that you may place it around your neck."

"And why would I wish to do that?"

"Because it will prevent you from sharing the fate of the unfortunate Mr. Thomas Gregson. The hamsa protects against the evil eye. It will save you from falling under almost any known form of enchantment."

"Even yours?" I asked, in a nervous jest. In truth, I was only half listening because my heart had begun to beat at a rapid pace. I had not seen the Lady Hypatia, Holmes's immortal tutor, since she bid us farewell at the docks some weeks before. I had hoped to forge a connection with her---as a good friend, and perhaps, in time, even more---for I had not been so taken with a woman since I fell in love with my dear Mary. I had felt dead to world, to all enticements of romance, until I met the Lady Hypatia and learned her story. Eternal, insightful, courageous, she had reawakened my love.

But then I had lost my memory of her, and when it returned I was shamed by my feelings. Who was I to offer even friendship to her? And on our return from America, a magical picture had reminded me, with painful clarity, that it was my beloved Mary who still held my thoughts, who controlled my soul.

"Watson," Holmes said, none too gently, "if you are finished stewing over your obsession with my tutor, I shall answer your question."

I had no need to ask him how he had known. I had long since accepted that I was transparent to the man. A simple nod sufficed.

"The hamsa is a warding charm. It will deflect magical energy and nullify all enchantments, even ones that are not purposefully evil. No wizard or witch dares to touch such a device. That is why you must hold it." I saw a flicker of amusement on his face as we passed a gas lamp. "Were I to attempt to examine it, I would suffer a rather nasty burn on my fingers. I prefer to spare those delicate digits for torture in my chemistry experiments."

"If you know so much," I said, more peevishly than I intended, "why must you seek the Lady's advice?"

"Have you not noticed the strange glyphs on the hamsa, Watson? They are common to the period of the Library of Alexandria, in the time of the Lady's work there."

"So you wish her to read them to you?"

"I have little interest in the wording. But I will be very interested in why the Lady Hypatia gave such a device to Thomas Gregson---for that is the only way he could have acquired it."

Chapter Eleven

"Poor Master Thomas," the Lady Hypatia whispered. "I did warn him."

Holmes settled into a chair before a massive oaken desk carved with mythological creatures. Dragons and griffins, some with jewels for eyes, seemed to glare at us as we sat before their mistress. All around her were boxes and jars, great scrolls supported on ivory posts, and tapestries that, when watched closely, appeared to move, their sewn figures cavorting in a slow, stately dance. This was no ordinary office or study, but the heart of a great, yet most secret archives. Tucked deep beneath the streets of London, the Library of the Arcane housed the largest collection of the world's magical documents and artefacts. Its guardian, the immortal woman who, centuries before, had won fame as a mathematician and philosopher, was as beautiful and serene as I remembered. Her ginger hair was loose around her shoulders, and she wore a simple white gown in the style of the Greek muses.

"And the hamsa was your gift to him," Holmes said.

"Yes. I advised him to keep it with him always. But I feared, even as I departed, that he considered me nothing more than a sad and deluded woman, perhaps driven a bit insane by my injuries."

A flick of her fingertips indicated the webbing of scars that covered her exposed arms and neck. In 415 AD she had been torn apart by a Christian mob in the great Library of Alexandria, only to be resurrected to immortality by the last of the Egyptian magicians. Her face alone was spared the wounds. Now it was clouded with melancholy.

"Why are men so foolish?" she said. "If he had worn it, as I suggested, perhaps none of this would have occurred."

"Tell us the circumstances," Holmes directed. "I doubt that you visited his shop out of mere curiosity."

The Lady looked up. "You know that I have my sources in the world above. From time to time, a manuscript, document, or artefact is found that would be much safer if hidden in the Library of the Arcane."

I grasped her meaning immediately, recalling our previous visit to her chambers. She had entered a vault filled with books and documents, from which the most horrific growls and screams had emerged. Indeed, there were some texts for which the world was not prepared.

"Two months ago, I learned that Thomas Gregson had acquired the lost pages of the Devil's Bible."

At the announcement, Holmes sat up in his chair and scowled at our hostess. "Why did you not tell me such a thing was in London?"

The Lady favored my friend with a cool look. "I will thank you not to take that tone with me, Master Sherlock. Once, I resolved to alert you to every mystery and movement within the Shadows, and you told me that you had abandoned this dark world forever and did not wish to be disturbed in your more important work. I merely considered myself abiding by your rather pointed request."

Holmes had the good graces to give a chagrined nod. Though I felt foolish for asking, I risked their contempt and confessed my ignorance.

"How can the Devil have a Bible?"

The Lady Hypatia turned, favoring me with a lovely smile. "In the year 1229, a Bohemian monk named Herman the Recluse was sentenced to die for breaking his vows. Desperate to save his life, he swore to his abbot that he could, in one night, write a book that would contain not only the scriptures, but all of human history and knowledge as well. Amused by this clearly impossible offer, the abbot locked the monk in his cell. The monk labored madly, but to no avail, and at the last hour he offered his soul to Satan if the Devil would complete the work. That morning, when the cell was opened, the monk presented his superior with a masterpiece which contained not only all of holy writ and human wisdom, but a grotesque self-portrait of the Devil."

"That is the legend," Holmes grumbled. "The facts are these: a tremendous book, more properly known as the *Codex Gigas*, was the prized possession of a series of Bohemian monasteries throughout the middle ages until it was purchased for Emperor Rudolf II. The Swedes seized it as plunder in 1648, and for generations it rested in their Royal Library in Stockholm. In 1697 there was a great fire in that library and the *Codex* was saved only by being tossed from a window."

The Lady Hypatia held up a finger. "Allow me to finish! This book is very large and heavy, so it is not surprising that a bystander was nearly killed when the volume struck him. In the confusion, a dozen pages fluttered away. Rumor among the Shadows held that these pages were the most dangerous of all, for they contained an incantation that no other magical tome possessed---the spell that could create a Legion of the Damned."

"More zombies?" I whispered, remembering those terrible hours when all the dead of London seemed to be rising and stalking us. The Lady shook her head, and spoke in a quiet voice that chilled my blood.

"Not mindless zombies, but an army of wraiths united with mortal forms. Smart, strong and vengeful, they could be led by a wizard and would be impossible to defeat without divine intervention. Doctor, do you remember the stories of the war in Heaven that drove Lucifer into Hell? A Legion of the Damned, it is said, could unleash that same war here on earth."

I glanced at Holmes, only to find his brows drawn down and lips tightly compressed. A slight nod urged the Lady to continue.

"I knew that mankind would be safer if those missing pages of the Devil's Bible---or *Codex Gigas* if you prefer---were safely under lock and key in my vaults. So I braved the indignities of the mortal world by donning a ridiculous gown complete with corset and bustle and journeyed to the shop, presenting myself as an ordinary customer. I was determined to acquire the pages. But Thomas Gregson refused to sell them to me."

"Did he know what he had?" I asked.

The Lady Hypatia's ginger brows came together. "I believe that he knew it was a valuable curiosity; he told me that another client, a Frenchman, had bid high for them."

"The conjurer Etienne Lellouche?" Holmes asked.

"I do not know," the Lady answered. "Master Gregson was the soul of discretion. He was proud to have acquired such an important document. But he did not strike me as being a man aware of the existence of the Shadows. Rather, he was a victim of the gentle madness of a true collector. I had the strong suspicion that he rarely parted with any item in his sad little shop."

"Tell me, Madame," Holmes said, "since you have viewed the pages, are they all that the legends have claimed?"

The Lady rose from her chair, rubbing her arms together as if a sudden chill had raced through the room. "I had only a few minutes to study them. Still, I saw some of the most hideous incantations ever written, including one for binding a wraith to a corpse." She smiled slightly. "But if Lucifer did pen those spells, then the Archfiend has atrocious handwriting."

"How much did you offer Gregson for the pages?" Holmes asked.

"A price far above their value to any antiquarian. But still he refused to sell them to me. So I begged him that if he would not sell them, would he at least protect himself with the hamsa. I insisted that the pages were evil and that they would act as a magnet to malignant forces. He accepted the gift of the talisman, but I could see in his expression that he thought me a silly woman." She turned with a sharp smack of her hand to her desk. "Indeed, Master Sherlock, I should have summoned you and sent you to burgle his shop!"

"Had you done so, Thomas Gregson would still be alive," Holmes agreed, with what I found a distressing lack of chivalry. "And now it is apparent that Gilles de Rais---or at least his nefarious associate---has come into a most valuable possession."

"Gilles de Rais?"

Holmes told her of the summoning at Urian Hall and the horror that the artist had witnessed, as well as his own deductions as to the identity of the wraith. During the recitation, the Lady Hypatia drifted back to her seat. Her face turned ghastly white as Holmes spoke.

"By all the old gods---if you are correct in your deduction, and I believe that you are---if such an evil man should walk among us again..."

Holmes folded his arms. "I fear most of all for the children of London, the young boys, the street Arabs. My own Irregulars are just the fodder he would seek for his hideous pleasures. And now that he has the pages of the Devil's Bible, it will be far more difficult to stop him."

The Lady Hypatia considered Holmes for a long moment and then, bit by bit began to smile. He glared at her, as if he hardly found her expression appropriate to the moment.

"Master Sherlock, do you take me for a total fool?" she asked.

"Of course not!"

"I knew I could not allow such powerful objects to be free. But I could not steal all the pages from under the nose of their rightful owner. Nor could I break into his house and seize the collection, for I lack your criminal talents in such matters. But as I considered the articles before me, I found them rather like a bomb primed to go off. What would you have done in such a predicament, if faced with a ticking explosive?"

"I would defuse it, of course."

The Lady opened a drawer of her desk. She removed a long sheet of paper, unfolding it for us. I saw crabbed handwriting, along with images of circles, stars, and mythical creatures on its surface.

"I developed a distressing fit of coughing," the Lady Hypatia said, "and asked the kindly Mr. Gregson for a cup of water. He ran in the back to get it, and while he was pouring I removed this page and slipped it into my purse. It seemed to me the most dangerous of all the pages that I had read. Fortunately, the proprietor did not spot his loss and I escaped with my prize."

Even as she spoke, Holmes was peering over the document. He whipped his head up, eyes gleaming.

"You have done well, Madame. This is the spell for creating the Legion of the Damned."

"Ah, a compliment. How rare."

"I will need this page."

"No," she said, so firmly that we were both taken aback. "It will never leave these rooms. Master Sherlock, I trust you, but the world is a wicked place. If this wraith somehow manages to take a human form using the pages from the Devil's Bible, he will soon be aware that his collection is incomplete. He will seek to rectify that loss, and you know what he is capable of, should that happen."

"Do you think I would give this spell to him?"

"Not willingly. But you are half mortal, and despite what you wish to pretend, you have a heart. You care for those close to you. I will not allow you to fall into the position of being extorted." She took the paper and put it back in the drawer. "It is for your own good that I retain it here."

"You place yourself in danger."

She shook her head. "The Library is well warded. No one can enter without my permission. There is no safer place for this document to be kept."

"But what should we do now?" I asked.

She arched an eyebrow at me. "Is it not obvious, Doctor? You and your companion must find the wraith of Gilles de Rais and the man who aids him. Surely, Master Sherlock," she added, lowering a teacher's reprimanding gaze at my friend, "that is not a task beyond your abilities?"

Chapter Twelve

"I agree, Watson! We should pay a visit to Professor Steele, immediately."

"We should?" I sputtered. It was the following day and we had just finished our luncheon in a restaurant on the Strand. True to her word, Mrs. Hudson had departed after breakfast in search of the mysterious doll. Less than an hour later, Holmes had received a reply to his telegrams. He dropped to the sofa, and with a grunt of disgust, waved the paper in the air.

"I have confirmed the name of our opponent. My pride in having deduced his identity is, however, tempered by the thought of how formidable an adversary he will be."

"You know it is Gilles de Rais who was freed from Hell? How?"

"And inquiry to my colleagues in the French police force," Holmes said. "One of the strange side-effects of calling forth a wraith is that whatever remained of that individual's mortal corpse will flare and burn the moment his soul slips out of Hell. This way, an evil wraith can never return to his own body."

"But you said that the wizard was burned alive in 1440."

"Not completely," Holmes answered, with a dry and humorless laugh. "Nobility has its privileges, Watson, and our subject was a French baron. Before his remains were completely consumed, they were pulled from the fire and given to 'four ladies of rank' for burial. They interred him in a rather unremarkable chapel in Nantes, near the site of his execution. According to my source, this chapel has recently been set ablaze, nearly consumed by a conflagration that originated from deep within its vaults. The authorities, of course, suspect anarchists."

After this remarkable announcement, Holmes became uncommunicative, answering my inquiries with distracted grunts. It took some effort to coax him out of our rooms and into a decent restaurant. Over our meal, I told him of my adventure with the Great Maskelyne at the Lyceum Theatre, purely in an attempt to amuse him and draw him out of dark thoughts. At first he seemed to be hardly listening, but when I described the way the actors' bodies appeared to be compromised of colored glass, he began to be more intrigued. He peppered me with questions about each performer, especially the ones cast as Julius Caesar and Marie Antoinette. By the end of my tale he was energized and ready to take up a new line of investigation. "What can Professor Steele tell us?" I asked.

"Nothing of Gilles de Rais, I fear. But she can be of assistance in other ways."

"How so?"

"It occurs to me that we are at a disadvantage. The task I have set before Mrs. Hudson is a desperate gamble, unlikely to succeed. We cannot be everywhere at once, and even the Irregulars, swift of foot and bright of eye as they are, cannot observe the secret workings of the Shadows. Nor would I put them at risk, knowing the nature of our villain." He folded his napkin and signaled to our waiter. "But there are those who can be everywhere, quite without peril, and I will make use of them."

With that cryptic remark, we were off. We arrived at the Lyceum Theatre, where a nervous manager immediately responded to Holmes's card and his request to speak to the featured entertainer.

"It is good to see you again, Mr. Holmes," he said, as he led us through the warren of rooms behind the stage, "I have not forgotten how quickly you cleared up that bad business for us last year. But I must warn you that Professor Steele is a bit...*temperamental.*"

"I have yet to know a woman who was not," Holmes said.

"Ah, so true," the man agreed with a weak laugh, "but she has certain *requirements* in her contract. For example, we are not to disturb her in the hour before her performance. And all the equipment below the stage must remain covered and locked in trunks. None of our stagehands are allowed to assist. How such a rather---ah---*Junoesque* lady manages to set it up, all alone, is quite beyond me! But I will not argue with the box office receipts, which are almost as sizable as her...ahem, here we are." He gestured to the room at the end of the hall. "I will be pleased to make introductions."

Holmes held up his hand. "I would prefer to speak to Professor Steele alone. It is a confidential matter, related to a most distressing case."

The manager nodded. "Very well. And you must get to the point, I fear, for there is barely an hour before show time and she is most insistent on her schedule for preparation."

"Do not worry," Holmes said, in his most placating tone, "I would not think of making the lady late for her matinee."

With an anxious bob of his head, the manager retreated. The moment he turned the corner, Holmes snapped his fingers at me.

"Do you have your notebook?"

"I am never without it," I said.

"Good old Watson!" Holmes gave a silent clap of his hands. "You are ever reliable when improvisation is required. You are now no longer Dr. John Watson; from this moment on, you are Mr. James Williams, a reporter for the *New York Times*."

Holmes reached into his jacket and withdrew a small leather case. He handed me a calling card. I had half expected it to be one of his enchanted ones that changed title at will, but this looked ordinary enough. It bore the stated name and designation.

"Do you suppose you could manage an American accent?" Holmes asked. My loud snort gave him his answer. "Not necessary, I confess, but it would have been the crowning touch."

"What do you want me to do?"

"Conduct an interview. Delay Professor Steele with ridiculous questions until she tosses you out on your ear."

"For what purpose?"

"To make her angry and therefore careless. Follow her when she leaves. I will see you in the final act."

With no further instructions, Holmes turned and disappeared down the hall. I took a deep breath and knocked on the door.

"Yes?" The harsh voice was better suited to a roustabout than an actress. "Who is it?"

I made a quick check of the name on the card. "James Williams. I am a reporter, Madame."

She opened the door, filling the entire portal with her fleshy frame. Up close, I saw that she was an even plainer woman than she appeared on stage. Her frizzled hair hung in a limp braid and her eyes were a sickly shade of green. She had applied only a dash of make-up, revealing large and angry blemishes on her skin. She peered at me myopically through half-moon spectacles.

"Go away. I don't have time for an interview."

"Madame, please. My readers in Philadelphia are anxious to hear of your great London success."

I thrust my card forward. She blinked down at it.

"Philadelphia? It says here you are from the *Times*, in New York."

"Of course. Forgive me, Madame, I misspoke because...because I was so taken with your beauty."

She rolled her eyes, clearly unconvinced. "Oh very well, but I only have time for a question or two."

I stepped forward eagerly. Her dressing room was relatively small and bare, hardly the chamber that one would expect to be assigned to a leading lady. I noted an unusual detail, a plethora of large books piled high on a side table.

"Well?" the sizable actress demanded, when I allowed myself to be distracted by attempting to read the titles on the spines. I gathered little except they were works of history. "Ask your questions."

I muddled through what I hoped would be the proper lines of a journalistic inquisition, asking her about her origins and how long she had trod the boards. She answered by rote, giving me no more information than was contained in her opening monologue. At the same time, she worked rapidly to paint her face and sweep her hair up with pins.

"That's enough, I think," she said, just as I began to inquire whether she liked the London weather and how the Lyceum compared to other theatres where she had performed. "Please leave now."

"But I have more questions!" I protested.

"And I have a matinee to prepare for." She gestured at her rack of clothing. "I must dress."

"Oh, of course. I could wait behind that screen."

"What an impertinent fellow you are!"

"But my readers, they want to know more. Please Madame, take pity on them."

"Out! You must get out now!"

"Just a few more minutes."

She rose in a rush, the long velvet cord of her dressing gown snapping like a lion's tail. "Must I call for aid? I'll have you arrested if you don't leave this instant!"

I stumbled to the exit, all apologies and awkward bows. She slammed the door in my face, nearly breaking my nose. Remembering Holmes's order, I found a broom closet along the hall and slipped into it. A few minutes later, Professor Steele emerged from her dressing room, stalking down the corridor in a fury. She had donned her academic gown and its black folds gave her the appearance of a classical witch. I waited until she turned the corner then gave pursuit, trailing her at a distance. As the manager had suggested, she went immediately to the area below the stage. It was a dark and gloomy place, filled with old props and scenery, lit only by two flickering oil lamps. Stealthily, I ducked behind a collection of shields and swords. I expected to see her begin to assemble her equipment, but instead she merely paced before her covered boxes with her fingers placed to her lips.

"Damn that man," she muttered. "Steady...steady. Must think. Who shall we give them today? Cleopatra, perhaps? Attila the Hun? It's been some time since William Wallace, perhaps we should dust him off again. Drat that idiot for breaking my concentration...very well. Let us set our program."

I looked to the boxes, once again expecting her to begin to open them. Instead, to my astonishment, three streams of vapor rose from the floor. I gaped as the streams took the forms of two men and one woman, all of them dressed in antique clothing. I recognized none of them.

"Cleopatra?" the female form demanded. "She is rather cliché by now. Mary, Queen of Scots would be a better choice, I think."

"And I'm not doing Attila again. Where's the honor in stalking around the stage and roaring? A barbarian is an insult to my art!" the taller of the men argued. "Let me perform Tamburlaine instead, at least he has the merits of being classical."

The second man shook his head. "I should have Tamburlaine. I'm tired of spilling my guts in Wallace's finale."

"He's mine," the first man replied, with a snarl.

"Just because you played him on stage does not make you an authority on his life. And you are much too tall to be authentic!"

"Gentleman," the professor sighed, rubbing her hand to her forehead. She wore the expression of a mother exasperated with her quarreling children. "Enough of this! You will do as I tell you."

"Indeed," a sardonic voice interrupted, "for all the world is a stage---and for some the drama never ends."

Chapter Thirteen

Professor Steele whirled around. The figures winked out of existence as Sherlock Holmes stepped forward. A pale golden light emerged from the head of his cane, casting an eerie halo around his figure, so that he appeared almost as unearthly as the departed forms.

"Most ingenious, Professor. Unable to summon the actual spirits of history's illustrious personages, you have created characters for them. Watson, do join us," he called, signaling for me to enter the enchanted circle of light. "This lady holds the key to questions that the readers of your stories might like answered."

The stout woman looked back and forth between us. "I should have known! I was warned there would be debunkers, but I was expecting Maskelyne, not you."

Holmes showed teeth. "I am flattered to be placed on par with such a notable illusionist. Indeed, he would be most interested in your performance and could devise appropriate challenges."

"Are you threatening me?" she hissed.

"I am merely laying the groundwork for a request. I need your assistance."

She scowled. "In what way?"

"You are clearly a gifted medium, or, to use the Shadows term, a summoner. You can call wandering spirits to you and bind them to your will. How is it that you came upon the idea of calling up actors?"

The lady took a seat in a prop throne, leveling an imperious look at Holmes. "I was raised in the Dock Street Theatre of Charleston," she said, "the oldest playhouse in America. I discovered my abilities when I was young. This should not surprise you."

"It does not," Holmes agreed. "Mortals consider theatrical folk among the most superstitious in the world. But we know it is merely their closer connection to the Shadows. After all, they spend their lives in a world that is often a dream."

The lady frowned, but at Holmes's gesture she continued to speak. "Last year, while we were touring in England, my parents were killed and I found myself penniless. But I was able to convince my ghostly friends to take me on as their manager. Everyone sees spirits these days, so why not allow them to believe they are seeing the spirits of their heroes and idols? The show must go on."

"Holmes," I said, "how did you know they were the ghosts of actors and not the ghosts of Caesar or Marie Antoinette?"

My friend could not suppress a look of arch amusement. "Because you are such an excellent reporter, Watson! The clue was in your description of the characters on stage. I know my history better than our self-declared *Professor* does. Julius Caesar was not a man with a lush head of curly hair---he was nearly bald when he was assassinated. And Marie Antoinette never proclaimed that the poor of her nation should eat cake. These are fables that the true spirits of the dead would have balked at presenting. Ghosts may be bound to a summoner, but they cannot be forced to be anything other than what they were in life. An actor, of course, can be ordered to perform to his director's specifications."

"You have the truth of it," Professor Steele said. "But what exactly do you want?"

"I want you to summon the five restless spirits of Whitechapel and bind them to me," Holmes said. "I need them to search for a wraith and his companion."

The lady immediately shook her head. Fear replaced arrogance in her tone. "Those are rather hard spirits, Mr. Holmes. I have seen them but once, and I would not willingly seek their company again."

"You have only to arrange a meeting between us. Summoners have an advantage over wizards when it comes to commanding ghosts," Holmes said.

"And you will persecute me with debunkers if I do not?"

Holmes did not answer the question. He merely considered her, and after a long moment she wilted under his gaze.

"I promise you, Madame," he said at last, "that I mean you and your enterprise no harm. As long as you do not seek to convince the grief-stricken that you carry messages from lost loved ones, I will not speak out against you. All entertainers are, to a degree, blatant frauds, so there is no need to single you out for punishment."

"But who is it that you seek?" she whispered. "Who is so vile that you would need the bloody five of Whitechapel for your quest?"

Holmes stepped forward and whispered to her. I started to join them, but felt a tap upon my shoulder.

I turned and found myself face to face with the three ghosts. I babbled before I could stop myself.

"Who are you?" I asked. The man clad in the blue coat of an eighteenth century dandy executed a polite bow.

"I am David Garrick."

"And I Edmund Kean," his companion said, with a toss of his dark hair. He had the look of an eccentric, with a touch of madness to his eyes. Meanwhile, the lady favored me with a lascivious smile, twirling a golden curl around one finger. Her velvet dress was loose, and cut to such depths that her stunning *décolletage* was visible.

"And you are?" I asked, when she seemed inclined to be coy.

"Can you not guess? In life I was Nell Gwyn, actress and lover of His Majesty King Charles II."

Kean chuckled. "You see why he was called the Merry Monarch now, I take it? Who wouldn't be merry with such a fine wench as Nell in his bed?"

"Watson!"

Holmes stood beside me. "Our business here is finished. Let us depart."

"But the ghosts-"

"May continue to trod the boards in peace. Meanwhile, we must return home. We have our own part in this drama to prepare for."

Chapter Fourteen

"I feel ridiculous," I said, staring at my image in the mirror. Holmes had spent most of the early evening transforming me with his putty and greasepaints, and now I barely recognized myself beneath a layer of false hair and sea-carved crinkles in my skin. The jacket I wore reeked of the ocean, of salt and sweat and fish. I grimaced and turned away from the unfriendly glass, walking back to our shared chamber. "Do I have to be a sailor? I look worse than any Jack Tarr and I smell as fresh as last week's catch."

"I wished to honor your love of the sea," Holmes called from his room, and I could hear the amusement in his voice. "Though a true corsair is hard to find these days, and I doubted you would really wish to struggle with a peg-leg or a parrot." He emerged and had I not been accustomed to his great skills at changing his entire persona, I would have gasped in surprise. A redheaded, scar-faced fiend with a white-filmed eye and several rotten teeth had replaced my handsome friend.

"I have never seen you uglier," I stated, quite without humor.

"I will take that as a high compliment," Holmes said, winking his unaffected eye. "This smacks of a lark to you, I see."

I shrugged. "I hardly understand the need for such pretense, if we are merely meeting the spirits you have recruited to your cause."

"Nor would I require it, except that my last case took me to these same regions and, should I be recognized there, eluding assassination would require more energy than I wish to expend."

"You could always cast a glamour," I reminded him, thinking of a previous case and a powerful witch who could change her appearance entirely. Holmes shook his head.

"Likewise, a rather unnecessary supply of reserves would be drained to maintain that illusion. I think my theatrical arts will serve the purpose."

I chuckled at this bit of vanity. What did it say about Holmes, that he far preferred to demonstrate his mastery of make-up and costume, rather than cast a single spell? He was surely the most reluctant wizard the Shadows had ever produced. He clapped a disreputable cap to his head and led the way down the stairs, whistling the *Spanish Ladies* shanty as we descended. Just as he reached for the door it opened, revealing Mrs. Hudson on the threshold. She gave a cry of alarm and threw her hands to her face.

"Oh good heavens! How utterly frightful you are! And I have half a mind not to ever help you again," she scolded. Holmes raised a brushy eyebrow.

"So your investigation has borne fruit?"

"Well it has certainly given me blisters from walking all over London," our landlady huffed as she shooed us back into the vestibule. "I did find the store that sold the doll, but I was nearly arrested for my troubles!"

Holmes quickly pried the story from her. The doll had been on display in the window of Potts's Toys and Novelties, but almost a month before the window had been smashed and the doll, along with a substantial sum from the company cash box, had disappeared. Mrs. Hudson's precise description of the vanished plaything aroused a clerk's suspicions, and a Scotland Yard detective had been summoned.

"Bless my soul, it was Inspector Lestrade who arrived, and he vouched for my good character! How he laughed! But had it been anyone else they would have slapped the darbies on me! No, no, I won't hear your apologies---I just need a spot of tea to settle my nerves. Off with you!"

Not for the first time, I wondered if we would find our possessions on the street when we returned. Holmes digested Mrs. Hudson's information as we settled into the cab.

"Intriguing. Our culprit clearly was in need of money as well as the doll. And the timing fits. Potts's store is, as I recall, only half a block from Paddington Station. If our villain arrived on the train from Reading in the aftermath of the fire at Urian Hall, then he could..."

Holmes lapsed into silence, chewing on a pipe. I knew better than to make further inquiries. If I had learned nothing else from my time with him, it was to be patient. He would share his thoughts only when the moment pleased him.

We disembarked five blocks from our destination, as Holmes declared a need to stretch his legs. Whitechapel was, as always, a dreary and depressing place to me. Some have surmised that it was nothing but a warren of vice, that every dwelling was a brothel or a gambling den. In truth, it was a place of industry as well as squalor, where people eked out their living by doing the filthiest jobs imaginable. Men in bloodstained aprons walked past, for this was a region of slaughterhouses. Children played in the gutter, staring at us with hollow-eyed desperation. Many of them would never venture past this quarter, never know that life could be purer and happier. This was a world of common boarding houses, where men and women alike slept leaning over ropes rather than in beds, where life was cheap and often meaningless, and no amount of charity or government work could change its squalor.

We passed a small group of well-dressed men and women. I elbowed Holmes, inquiring as to why they would be in this section. They looked more like a theater party than charity workers.

"'Slumming,' Doctor. It is all the rage, to venture into Hell to look at the damned. Now, silence if you please. We have reached our rendezvous."

It was a pub called *The Hanged Man*, as desperate and wretched a place as one might ever see in the bowels of the city. Holmes led me inside and we elbowed our way through the crowd. They were hardly a jolly crew, despite the racket of conversation and the popular tunes being banged out on an ill-tuned piano in the corner. Most of the patrons were people who drank not for pleasure, but simply to dull the pain of their existence. Holmes signaled to the bar keeper, who in turn opened a panel behind his counter, hustling us inside. Within was a small room with a table and two chairs. The bartender put two dirty glasses before us, along with a bottle of gin, and quickly departed.

"A drink?" Holmes asked.

"I would think it might be poison, in a place like this."

Holmes chuckled. "This is one of the calmer pubs in Whitechapel. And the proprietor, as you may have guessed, is an old friend of mine. Well, perhaps friend is too strong of a word. I saved him from the gallows twice; what type of relationship does that establish, I wonder?"

For half an hour we chatted amiably. Or, rather, Holmes regaled me with stories while I nervously watched the panel, expecting at any minute that a band of cutthroats would enter to put an end to my friend's celebrated career.

"Watson," he said, sharply. He motioned to my glass.

It was covered in a rim of frost. I started to touch it, but Holmes gave a harsh shake of his head. His breath smoked. He turned around, directing his comments to the empty air.

"Welcome, ladies," Holmes said to the suddenly frigid atmosphere around us. "Please, for the comfort of my associate, I ask you to show yourselves."

With that strange request, five figures appeared in the space between our table and the secret door. Four of them were common drabs, women of the street in tattered skirts and soiled aprons, one with a saucy bonnet upon her head. The last in the group was a younger woman, of some spirit and brighter looks, with golden hair worn loose around her shoulders.

All of them were, as the ghosts of the theater had been, made of vapors and transparent, like images drawn on colored glass. Yet they were somehow real, substantial, and vivid in their details, from the buttons on their boots to the scars on their faces. The tallest of the bunch removed a pipe from the blackened stubs of teeth.

"What do you want of us?"

"Assistance," Holmes said. Without preamble, he told them of the resurrection of the wraith and how Gilles de Rais and his mysterious assistant were afoot in London.

"You can go where others cannot," Holmes said. "I need these men tracked down, so that I may deal with them."

"You cannot command us," the smallest of the assembly stated. "Our whoring days are done!"

"And why should we help you?" the woman in the bonnet asked. "You have done nothing for us. We walk because there is no justice. Provide it for us!"

Holmes shook his head. "The one you seek is beyond my grasp."

"Then we shall not aid you," the oldest harridan snapped. "We have answered the summons, but we shall not be ruled by any of the living. You will not force us to do this thing!"

I felt a prickle along my neck. I noted how the youngest of the party was considering me. She plucked a long ringlet from her shoulder and twisted it around her finger as Nell Gwyn had done, smiling at me in a manner I found shockingly intoxicating. I was uncertain of how to respond. Did one dare to show attention, or even admiration, to a ghost? I offered what was surely an anxious, embarrassed grin. In response, she giggled.

"Mary!" the pipe-bearing woman snapped.

"Would it be too much to help them, just a little? They seem very nice," she said, and I thrilled to the slight French accent of her words.

"We are a sisterhood," the eldest stated, "we must work as one."

The young woman frowned and shook her head. The tallest motioned for them to come together, and as they huddled in a pack, whispering to each other, I looked to Holmes. For an instant I thought I saw a strange and alien emotion cross his face. It was a look of regret, tinged perhaps with a modicum of guilt. At last, after much private consultation, the women turned to face us.

"We will aid you, Sherlock Holmes," the spirit with the pipe said. "But only when you agree to give us the justice we require, that we might rest in peace."

"Shall we show him what we can do because we do not rest?" the ugliest one asked, putting a hand to her bodice. The other three harridans followed suit, clawing at buttons and scarves.

Holmes jumped to his feet. "Away with you!"

The women laughed and disappeared into the ether. Holmes settled back and took a long swallow of gin.

"What did they wish to show us?" I asked.

"Something you truly did not wish to see," Holmes stated. I was shocked to see him so unnerved. He fished for his cigarette case, nearly spilling its contents on the table. "This was an error on my part. I should have known better than to summon this quintet."

"But who are they?"

"You did not recognize them?" Holmes asked.

"Of course not. Holmes, I am no walking encyclopedia of crime, much less of wraiths, fairies, and spirits."

He hoisted his glass in salute. "They are Mary Ann Nichols, Annie Chapman, Elizabeth Stride, Catherine Eddowes and Mary Jane Kelly---the victims of Jack the Ripper."

Chapter Fifteen

For a long moment I simply stared at Holmes. How well I recalled those dark days in the autumn of 1888, when a fiend carved his way through the slums of London. The newspapers could talk of little else. The speculation had been endless; there were whispers that the villain was not a local tough, but a dapper toff or even a nobleman. Once, at my club, a member had argued rather passionately that the killer was none other than Prince Eddy. Ridiculous, I had said at the time, though oddly enough the man who stated that theory never returned to our ranks. I learned later than he had met with a terrible hunting accident only a few days after his remarkable monologue.

The memory brought back a shudder. I took a sip from my glass.

"I recall that both Lestrade and Gregson came to you, but you would not take the case."

"I was occupied with other matters, as you no doubt recall," Holmes said. "And, at that time, I was insistent on maintaining my exile from the Shadows."

"The Ripper was a supernatural creature?" I blurted.

"I did not say that," Holmes countered. "But the case was dark, with unnatural overtones, and I preferred to maintain a respectful distance from it."

I considered the implications of this statement. "Had you intervened, perhaps some of those women would not have died!"

"Perhaps," Holmes allowed. He turned to me, eyes narrowed. "Will you blame me for every murder I do not prevent, Watson? Do you think that my powers are so extensive I could stop all bullets or overpower each hand that holds a knife?"

"No," I answered, and perhaps the burn of the cheap liquor gave me courage to meet his gaze and speak my mind freely. "But I do think that sometimes you choose the battles that will bring you glory, rather than the ones that will serve mankind."

Holmes flinched, something I had never, to my recollection, seen him do. He was poised to make some rejoinder when a shout sounded outside our chamber. Breaking glass and a peppering of curses followed it. Holmes rose and, with a final gulp of gin, I followed him through the sliding panel.

A hatless, flush-faced man was standing at the bar drinking straight from a bottle, despite the bar keeper's loud protests. Several louts were shouting ribald encouragement. Overturned chairs and tables marked the newcomer's path to the counter, and several surly characters appeared to be rolling up their sleeves to do battle with him.

The man crashed the bottle down onto the bar, shattering it. "Give me another!" he screamed, seemingly unaware that the tender was reaching for a club, not a green glass containing more whiskey. "My God, the dead are walking tonight, give me a drink!"

"I promise you, Watson, I choose my battles very carefully," Holmes said. With that pronouncement, he took a swing at me. His fist connected with my jaw, and I tumbled backward onto a table. I flipped over to a chorus of happy shouts as a general melee broke out all around us. While I had seen my share of roistering in the army, I had never been thrust so unceremoniously into the fray. It took all my skills not to be pummeled into a pulp. I concentrated on making my way to the door, thinking that if Holmes had lost his mind and decided to put on a boxing exhibition for these wretches, he could jolly well prove his pugilistic abilities on his own. I slid through the doorway just as a neighborhood gang surged in, baying like excited hounds. I limped over to a lamppost and was gingerly testing a loosened tooth with my tongue when two of the most hideous doxies in Whitechapel reeled from the pub. One seemed sober enough, but the other was slobbering and gasping as if she had just been punched in the stomach.

"Be a good chap, Watson, and help me carry our new friend to safety," the taller of the women said as she staggered past me.

I blinked. Like a curtain falling, the image of wild curls, tattered shawls, and gathered skirts fell away, leaving Holmes and the drunkard in their wake. Holmes looked back and winked at me.

"A small glamour and not long held, but still---I find it exhausting. Some assistance, if you please?"

Truly, the man was intolerable. But long years of companionship sparked action, and I grabbed the other fellow's arm and threw it over my shoulder. Holmes steered us clear of the riot, not halting until we reached a quiet yard. Holmes kicked open the gate and helped me settle the nearly unconscious man on a doorstep.

"A thousand apologies, my dear Watson," Holmes said, holding up his hands. "I would have given you warning if I could, but immediate action was necessary. And I much prefer to conduct this interview in private, without the benefit of liquid refreshment."

The stranger moaned. Holmes knelt down and delivered a few sharp slaps to his cheeks. The man rallied enough to protest the treatment.

"Err now---blast your eyes---leave me alone! I have to get home. The dead are walking."

"Indeed, Mr. Joseph Martin?"

The man was instantly sober. He blinked at Holmes. "You know me. Who are you?"

Holmes sighed and ripped away the mop of ginger hair. He popped the bit of colored glass from his right eye. "I think you may recall me now."

"Sherlock Holmes," Martin gasped. "It's worth your life to be seen on these streets!"

Holmes smiled thinly as he made introductions. "Mr. Joseph Martin is a photographer by trade. He is the man the police call when they wish an image of a murder victim taken for identification purposes. A man with an unwavering gaze and a strong stomach, to be certain." Holmes scowled. "And not a man to be easily frightened. Tell me, sir, why do you think the dead are walking?"

"Because I have seen them. I never forget a face when he is put before my lens, sir. And I have seen his face on the street tonight. It is a face that should be six feet under the earth and food for worms."

"I do not believe you," Holmes snapped. The effect was immediate. Martin sat up and became even more impassioned in his speech.

"It is true, I swear it! Yesterday, they called me to the Dorset Street mortuary, to make a picture of a man who had hanged himself in a garret. A robust chap, once a handsome fellow, with yellow hair and shoulders so broad they had to turn him sideways to fit the casket. He was unknown to anyone, and I made three images. He was to be buried this morning, but tonight I saw him walking down Flower and Dean, as spry as you please."

"Perhaps he was not dead when you photographed him," I said, as it was the most sensible and reasonable explanation. The man whirled on me, his body trembling.

"I know the dead! I have taken more postmortem pictures than any man in London. But I tell you, this was a walking corpse…and he was not the first."

Holmes had risen and was turning way, but this addition drew him back. "Not the first? How many others?"

Martin rocked forward, drawing his knees to his chest. "At least two more, both from the Dorset Street mortuary. First it was a man who shot himself, and then it was a chap who took poison."

"Both unknown?" Holmes asked.

"Yes. That's why I was called in, no one had claimed them."

"And did you report this?"

"No. Folks would think me mad. Perhaps I am mad. Give me a drink---for God's sake, have pity on me and give me a drink!"

Holmes pressed a fist to his lips. "This makes many things clearer."

"I fail to see how," I muttered.

"The pieces of the puzzle come together," Holmes said, as if he had not heard my words. "Come, Watson, let us return to Baker Street."

"What about Martin?" I asked, feeling pity for a man reduced to the state of a wailing child by his terror.

Holmes scowled. Clearly, this problem did not interest him.

"Can you see him home?"

"I can."

"Excellent."

And with that brusque dismissal, my friend disappeared into the shadows.

Chapter Sixteen

I awoke late the next morning, in a rather foul humor. Holmes's punch had left a purplish bruise on my jaw and my head ached from the long night's weary journey. Ferrying Martin back to his residence had depleted the meager funds in my pocket, forcing me to walk most of the way back to Baker Street. As a result, I had taken only the briefest of naps, and cursed into my pillow when Holmes pounded on my door, ordering me out of bed.

I stared glumly at my reflection in the silver coffee pot. I had never before truly questioned my partnership with Holmes. I had shared his adventures, and their dangers, quite willingly. I prided myself on being an old campaigner. I had ignored the twinges of my old wounds and forgone the financial advantages of resuming a regular medical practice. I had, for so many years, built my life upon his.

Had I erred?

I blinked and became aware of another reflection in the bright surface before me. I turned, finding Holmes dressed and holding out a slip of paper.

"Watson, old friend...I need your assistance."

I was in no mood to give it. I glared at him until he coughed and cleared his throat, surely aware that an apology was necessary.

"I realize my actions toward you last evening were atrocious. And I confess you touched the rawest nerve I possess." He nodded, as if hearing an inner accusation. "It is true, I allowed the women of Whitechapel to die. At the time, I did not feel the case worthy of my attention or the risk I would take by using my Shadowborn skills to seek the killer. Now I have the opportunity to make amends, and to prevent the rise of a murderer who would make Jack the Ripper seem like a naughty schoolboy."

I started to object to his vanity. He thrust the paper forward.

"But I cannot do this without you."

The slip of foolscap hung between us. At last I reached out my hand and took it, unfolding it on the table. There was a name written on the paper.

"Do you know him?" Holmes asked.

I nodded and rose to fetch my coat.

**

"Tell me about Dr. Herman Bradley," Holmes said, as our cab made its way to London's East End.

"He was a fine physician," I said, "the top of his class from the University of London in 1870. They still spoke of him when I was a student there, sang the praises of his pioneering work in diseases of the mind. But his career was cut short by tragedy."

"Of what sort?"

"His wife and two young children were aboard the *Princess Alice.*"

Holmes acknowledged his recollection of the great disaster of 1878, when a pleasure craft had sunk in the Thames, with a heavy loss of life. "Such a tragedy would ruin a sensitive man."

"And it did. Bradley was, for a time, as insane as one of his patients. At last he rallied, but it was too late for his career." I twisted, studying my friend's face. "But how is he part of this?"

"Dr. Bradley is in charge of the Dorset Street mortuary, where Martin works and the photographs would have been made. You see the pattern, do you not?"

"Three suicides," I said.

"Four," Holmes corrected. "You forget the sad demise of Thomas Gregson."

"And you think they are connected?"

Holmes drummed his fingers on the head of his cane. "I am certain of it. The wraith is seeking to return to the land of the living. He must possess a body, one with a flown soul. And, without a doubt, he prefers a fresh body of a young and vigorous male. How does one obtain such a body? The young and vigorous are less likely to perish from illness, and the wraith would hardly desire a corpse brought low by an accident, missing arms or legs or even a head! No, Watson, the simplest and fastest way to obtain corpses with no untidy questions asked is to force them to commit self-destruction."

"Murder by suicide," I reflected. "But you said the wraith cannot cause harm."

"Indeed. But his assistant can. Do you recall Thomas Gregson's final words?"

A chill ran through me, as if ice had been poured into my blood. "Those eyes, those horrible eyes!"

"Mesmerism," Holmes said. "I think our villain has Shadows in his blood, and the Shadows give exceptional power to unique talents. Think of the music hall mesmerist who causes men to bark like dogs or sing nursery rhymes. Now enhance those abilities with the Shadows, so that the man can implant vicious suggestions in the minds of his victims. Quite frankly, I fear that the inspector's brother was a dead man the moment his client raised those dark glasses and gazed at him."

"So he finds men to enchant, ordering them to kill themselves. But why so many? Is Gilles de Rais not satisfied with the bodies he finds?"

Holmes shook his head. "Far from it. If the wraith could hold his spirit inside any of these bodies, he would no doubt be once again in the business of abusing and slaying young boys. But he has a particular problem."

"His spell is not working! Something has gone awry."

"Exactly." Our cab came to a halt. "Let us see what Dr. Bradley can tell us."

We disembarked at the door to what I took to be a stable. Holmes corrected me; this was the Dorset Street mortuary. I repressed a shudder as we entered, quickly pulling my handkerchief to cover my mouth. The dim interior reeked of carbolic acid, but that could not cover the smell of death and decay. Holmes seemed unaffected, and after a brief word with a sallow-faced attendant, who barely looked away from the penny dreadful he was reading, we entered the inner sanctum.

My eyes fell at once upon a stack of caskets along one wall. They were of all shapes and sizes, ready to receive the bodies of men, women, and children. One leaned upright, its lid beside it, revealing a tattered and faded lining of purple silk. The container had clearly been used before, judging by the stains on the fabric. I guessed such coffins could be rented for the journey to the grave, and afterward the body would be cast into the raw earth with nothing but a cheap shroud to protect it.

"If you're here about the old hag, it's dysentery, not the plague. No need to get your blue-bottle knickers in a twist."

The words came from a man who was bent over an examination table made from an old door placed on two sawhorses. He wore a heavy apron and his sleeves were rolled up. On one side was a medical bag and on the other a bottle of gin.

"We are not here about the old woman," Holmes said, his soft voice surprisingly sharp in the putrid air of the room, "but rather about the young men able to walk the streets of Whitechapel after they should have been buried."

The man turned. I recalled the picture of Dr. Herman Bradley in the hallway beside the surgical theater. We had all admired him, for he was a handsome man, with a prominent chin and clear eyes. Now his body was lean, his color toxic from drink, and unkempt grey side-whiskers jutted out like noxious moss upon his face. He squinted at my friend.

"I...I have no idea what you mean."

"Come now, Doctor, this will hardly do. I have a list of witnesses who will testify that men who have passed through this morgue as corpses are now walking the streets of London."

Bradley did not reply. He grabbed a rag from the table and began to wipe his hands.

"You may talk to me or to Inspector Tobias Gregson," Holmes said. "But I will warn you that the inspector has a personal interest in this case and will not be inclined to be merciful. You will get better terms from me."

"You have no witnesses," the physician snarled. "The dead do not shuffle around the streets."

"And how can you be certain?" Holmes asked, as politely as making an inquiry about the weather.

"Because *he* brings them back for me to bury."

The words hit me like a punch, but Holmes merely folded his arms. Bradley sighed and retrieved his bottle. Holmes stepped into his path when he tried to exit.

"Once last chance, Doctor. I think I will be more understanding of your needs. Gambling debts must be paid. A child you love must be supported."

I had no idea how Holmes knew these things, what clues he had gathered from the physician's attire and person, but he had clearly struck home. With a strangled cry Bradley dropped his bottle and buried his face in his hands.

"God help me, what have I done?"

Holmes took his elbow and guided him to the far corner of the room, insisting that he settle himself onto a stool. Bradley slumped forward, his hands dangling between his knees.

"It's all for the two of them, I swear. Charlotte and her mother. I can't marry my darling, she has a husband somewhere. But the girl is mine and I won't let her rot in this terrible place. I'd sell my soul for her, I would."

"Tell me about the man," Holmes said. "The one who buys the bodies."

"He's a strange fellow...he always wears dark glasses and his hair is long, tied up in a braid. He has the most peculiar accent, something eastern, I suppose, but twisted up with French, his words all broken." Bradley shuddered. "Even queerer, he carries a doll with him. Sometimes he seems to speak to it, like a living child. I've never seen anything like it, even during my days as an alienist."

"Did he give you his name?"

Bradley licked his lips. "He told me his name was Grigori Kirov and that he was a medical student and needed bodies for his research. He asked to be notified when a suicide was brought in. He was very specific. He only wanted young men, those with no families."

"And you sent for him after the bodies were photographed?"

"Yes. He came instantly, took the bodies from me. I felt there was no harm done as those unfortunates had no kith or kin, and my client paid well."

"You found nothing strange about this?" Holmes asked.

"It is not the first time I have been asked to supply a body to a medical student," Bradley admitted. "It was only the specificity that shocked me."

"But what of the inquest?" I asked, shocked by this perversion of justice. "Was there no investigation of these deaths?"

Bradley favored me with a look of near contempt. "No one cared about these wretches. Kirov gave me enough money to hush up the people who brought them in, and the police as well. Death is our trade in this part of London."

"Why did you have them photographed?" Holmes said. Bradley turned bloodshot eyes in his direction.

"Because I have some conscience, sir. I called Martin in, to make the pictures in case someone came looking for one of them, some time in the future. It would be easy enough to claim the man had already been buried in an unmarked grave, but at least a grieving friend would have the photograph as a memento. Just as I have mine."

He pulled a locket from a rough cord around his neck and clicked it open inside his chemical-stained palm. It revealed the image of a lovely woman and two small boys. Looking closer, I saw that the mother and her babes were lying together inside a coffin.

Holmes refused to be moved by the show of sentiment. "You say you have reburied the corpses."

"In each case, a day after the body was claimed, it was returned to my door. I was shocked at first; I would have supposed that a student would have disposed of the body in some other manner. In fact, the brazenness of it was offensive. But then I noted something puzzling, a mystery I tried to solve for myself and could not."

"The bodies showed no sign of decay," Holmes said.

"You...you are correct," Bradley murmured, giving my friend a look of astonishment. "They had not even passed into rigor. It was as if they had lived again and were freshly dead, even fresher than they had been when I first made their acquaintance. I confess I did a postmortem on this second visit, because I was certain the student had devised some diabolical form of re-animation. Surely I could determine what methods he had used, whether he had applied electricity, like the mad scientist of Mrs. Shelley's novel, or some marvelous chemical. Whatever he could do, I could replicate." When Holmes showed no sympathy, Bradley turned once again to me. "Imagine if I were the doctor who could cure death!"

"Then you would be the man who brought the greatest curse on the human race," I said, almost without thought. Bradley wilted and drooped, his hands going slack. The locket fell to the floor with a tinkling sound. Holmes demanded Kirov's address, and Bradley reluctantly scribbled it out. He turned to me as he passed the ragged note to Holmes.

"No doubt you are right. I would be condemned for interfering with the plans of God. And all my investigations brought me no closer, for when I opened the bodies I found nothing to give a clue to their

135

resurrection. When I removed their skulls, what I found was even more impossible."

Holmes seemed oddly intrigued. Bradley gave a rough cough.

"Their brains had been reduced to ash."

A sudden thud on the door gave us all a start. Bradley staggered to his feet and threw open the portal. The sleepy-eyed assistant stood there, waving his ragged novel toward the street.

"Another one brought back. Left in the cart."

It was unnecessary for Bradley to urge us to follow; Holmes was already ahead of him, shoving the attendant to one side. In the alley was a decrepit wagon filled with hay and broken bottles. Resting atop the debris was the body of a young man with his eyes wide and his mouth open to the heavens. Holmes put a hand to his throat and then tested the flexibility of an arm.

"Still warm," he whispered. "Not more than an hour dead. Is this the last body you sold?"

Bradley stood just inside the doorway, as if unwilling to face another consequence of his actions. "It is. The last of three."

Holmes studied the face of the deceased. Solemnly, he reached out and closed the young man's eyes. "Did you inform Kirov that his subjects were being photographed?"

"No," Bradley said.

"Then we are in luck. Sell no more," Holmes ordered. "Is that understood?"

Bradley nodded.

Chapter Seventeen

"Tell me, Doctor, did you enjoy the sport of tiger hunting during your sojourn in the East?"

We were once again ensconced in a hansom cab. I had expected Holmes to direct our driver to the address Bradley had provided, the place of residence of the mysterious wraith and his horrible companion. Instead, Holmes had asked the man to take us back to Baker Street. This sudden change in conversation was also rather unaccountable, considering the gravity of the case.

"Once," I allowed, "but I did not have any success at the pursuit. You may recall that the extent of my excitement came when a cub poked its head into my tent in the middle of the night."

"I thought it was a double-barreled musket that invaded your dwelling," Holmes said, "and that you dispatched it with the tiger cub."

I chuckled at his reference. All those years ago, in trying to impress my beautiful Mary, I had gotten the tale rather twisted. But why was Holmes making this inquiry now? Naturally, my friend answered my unspoken question.

"Because I wonder if you have ever watched a clever tiger, Watson. When the old *shikari* puts out the bait, staking the young goat in a clearing, the hungry and desperate juvenile tiger will come and is easily slaughtered by the hunter in the tree above him. But the mature tiger, older and more experienced, a master of cunning, senses that such an easy prize is not to be trusted. The striped fiend will hide and wait, ignoring the most piteous bleats of the goat, for he knows his enemy is near. He does not take the bait and he lives to hunt another day."

"What do you mean by this?"

"Simply that I am too old of a tiger to walk so blithely into a trap. But hello---driver, go around that vehicle, if you will. Watson, it seems we have a royal visitor."

A four-wheeler sat before our kerb. It was old, black, and as nondescript of a conveyance as had ever plied the London trade. The single horse was a scrawny bay, a nag only a few steps away from the glue factory. The driver was slumped on the box, arms folded and head down, taking a noonday nap. The windows of the carriage were open, revealing a single occupant. I was reminded of Miss Mary Sutherland, one of Holmes's former clients, as the lady inside the carriage wore a sizable hat and a feathery boa around her neck. Her solid face was as drab and unmemorable as her mode of transportation.

"Royal? You have a rather odd sense of humor, Holmes."

He winked as me as we descended just a few doors beyond our destination and began backtracking to the waiting carriage. "Have you put the hamsa around your throat?"

"Yes. I found a chain for it this morning."

"Indeed, I am gratified to learn that you have followed my suggestion. But now, if you would, remove the talisman from contact with your skin."

I pulled the little chain forward and laid the charm over my collar. Holmes lifted one hand, whispering words in his spidery language of magic.

The glamour affixed to the carriage dissolved and I saw it in its true form. It was made of an enormous silver shell with wheels of solid gold. The horse became a two-headed unicorn, with eyes that blazed fire and dark smoke emitting from its nostrils. The weary cabman was a pointed-eared elf lady, fair of face but bristling with muscles and holding a spear that she pointed aggressively in our direction. Holmes signaled for peace and moved to the side of the vehicle.

"Your Majesty," he said, giving a short bow, "what brings you to the neighborhood?"

It was Titania, the Queen of the Fae and, by extension, one of my friend's distant relations. Her purple hair floated around her face and her wings rested comfortably on pillows made of dandelions. As before, she was completely nude, her only adornments the bejeweled diadem which Holmes had restored to her on a previous adventure.

"Your business is with the lady inside, not with me," she said tartly. "Though I do hold you responsible for her grief. If this were the Court of Midsummer, I would summon you to face justice."

It was rare to see Holmes express true bafflement. "I have not caused harm to any lady."

"So you think. Don't stand here and gape! Go inside."

Holmes whirled. Uncertain of how one properly took one's leave from a fairy queen, I gave an awkward bow and hurried after him. Mrs. Hudson met us in the hall.

"There's a lady for you, sir. Poor thing, she's much too young to be a widow."

Holmes raced past her. I was at his heels, hearing Mrs. Hudson's harrumph at our rudeness.

The lady was in deepest mourning. She lifted her veil as we approached. My heart sank at the once beautiful, now haggard and drained face of Miss Simone.

"Mrs. Smythe," she corrected softly, when Holmes addressed her. "Even though I was a wife for less than an hour."

Holmes dropped into his chair. "Tell me what has happened."

"Robert...my love...returned to me the day after I came to you. Oh, it was wondrous, my joy at seeing him again. He would tell me nothing of where he had been.

Instead, he did the most remarkable thing! I am sure that you will doubt my sanity if I tell you but-"

"He drew a picture," Holmes said softly, "and took you through it."

"Yes! Oh, sir, you are so clever to have guessed it! It was a land of enchantments, of fairies and wee folk. I thought I was dreaming."

"Yet you returned to dirty old London," Holmes said, cutting off her potentially lengthy exposition of the delights of the Shadows. "Why?"

"Because we wished to marry. I had promised my mother, on her deathbed, that I would find a man to make an honest woman of me and I would marry in St. Monica's Church. I begged my darling to help me honor my promise, and reluctantly he agreed. He went back through the picture to make the arrangements and when he returned he was pale and shaken. He sat down to compose a message, and when it came time for us to depart the Shadow country for London, I saw him seal the papers into an envelope, which he placed in his jacket. I assumed it was merely some unfinished business he had, so I did not inquire further.

"We crossed back into London and made our way together to the church. Mr. Holmes, there was never a more handsome groom than my Robert, though I confess he was paler than I had hoped, and his eyes roamed restlessly around the sanctuary. Two of his friends stood as our witnesses, and they teased him a good deal about his nerves. But the vows were said and we went out of the church as husband and wife, to the hurrahs of our little band of merrymakers. It was then, as we were crossing the street, that it happened. It was a runaway cab---a black horse stampeding with no driver in the box. There was screaming and everyone leapt for the kerb. But Robert, he stood frozen, only at the very last second throwing out his hands. He was trampled by the horses and crushed by the wheels. We ran back to him, but he expired in my arms, unable to whisper even a single word of farewell."

The lady pulled a black-banded handkerchief from her sleeve, gently daubing her red-rimmed eyes. "That was yesterday. This morning one of my husband's relatives came to me. She told me she was his aunt and she asked questions as to how he died. I dared not tell her of the Shadow Lands and the fairies, lest she think me mad. I showed her the envelope from Robert's jacket, and she immediately recognized your name. She urged me to bring it to you without delay, and so here I am."

She passed the brown envelope to Holmes. He flipped it over, noting how carefully it was sealed with red wax. "You are unaware of its contents?"

"Completely, sir."

"That is for the best." Holmes rose, holding out his hand. "I am sorry for your loss, Madame. I had hoped the two of you would know many years of continued happiness."

"The memories of my last day with him will be my paradise," she whispered. "I only wish I knew how such an illusion was achieved. I was so sure I was in a fairy country."

Holmes moved to the window. "Be guided by your in-law's advice. The lady who waits for you will help you in ways that I cannot."

Mrs. Smythe smiled. "She is a very kind and gentle person. How I wish I had known her sooner. Thank you, Mr. Homes, for all that you have done."

Our former client made a sad but graceful exit from our rooms. I had restored the hamsa to my throat, so that when I looked through the window it was an ordinary four-wheeler to which the young widow was admitted.

"Imagine," Holmes laughed, "my wicked old soul-stealing aunt described as a kind and gentle person."

"Is the girl safe with Titania?"

Holmes nodded. "The fairies have a love of beautiful mortals. And, if my observational powers do not deceive me, another creature of the Shadowblood will make his or her appearance in some six months! Titania has a soft spot in her heart for the orphans of the Shadows. I am sure that at the proper moment she will drop her glamour and escort the expectant mother to the Midsummer Court."

"But why did Titania blame you for the girl's suffering?"

Holmes held up the envelope. "This seal has been broken; it reeks of fae magic to restore it to the impression of freshness. I think we will find our answer within."

Chapter Eighteen

Holmes opened the envelope and removed several folded pages. His eyes darted over the words, and then he thrust the documents to me with a command to read them aloud. I did so as he dropped into his chair, his palms pressed tightly together.

"'*Holmes*,'" the letter began, "*I write this in hopes that, when it reaches you, I will be on my honeymoon with my beloved Venus. I had half a mind to wash my hands of the matter, but then considered your goodness to me. Had you not forced me from my paintings, I might have cowered there until it was too late to make a life with the most wonderful woman who ever lived. For that I must both thank you and warn you of my unforgiveable betrayal.*

Beatrice insisted that our wedding be conducted in London, in the Church of Saint Monica. I would never have crossed the boundaries of the Shadows again, had it not been to please her. I returned via my new sketch and made my way around the metropolis, making the appointment with the priest, buying a ring, and hiring a room for the wedding breakfast, as well as alerting some of my friends to the time of the nuptials. It was this simple action that led me to misfortune and, I fear for you, an exposure to the greatest danger.

My friends prevailed upon me to indulge with them in an evening's jollification to mark the end of my bachelorhood. I felt I could not refuse, as I would never see them again. And so, in the wee hours of the morning, I found myself half-intoxicated, staggering through the streets of Whitechapel. Ned, my oldest and dearest companion, insisted that we visit a certain pub. I despair of recalling its name, though I believe there was some type of hound on its sign. I heard a clock strike two as we lurched through the door. The room was filled with revelers, but my gaze was drawn immediately to a man who was dancing upon a table. He kicked and squatted, his gyrations set to ribald cheers and great clapping. I noted that he was wearing a peasant blouse and loose trousers, and I assumed he was one of the many immigrants who have arrived like so much flotsam and jetsam on our shores. Just as we claimed seats for our party, I heard the man on the table shouting, in broken English, that his master would soon be free. That strange assertion caused me to look closer at the face of this drunken reveler.

You can only imagine my horror, Mr. Holmes, when I realized that he was the same man I had encountered at Urian Hall, the man Lellouche addressed as Mr. E. I was astonished to see that he had survived the fire. But even as I rose, it occurred to me that his survival implied an allegiance to the thing that had been conjured from the void. I turned to flee, but my intoxicated friends clutched at me, trying to hold me back, offering to buy me another pint. At last I threw them off and dashed for the door and freedom.

I halted, nearly falling, for there on the threshold was something unnatural and freakish. You may laugh, but I swear by my blood that it was a horror that caused me to scream and fall backward into the awkward arms of the other patrons. It was a doll---a child's toy, in the form of a little sailor boy---yet it radiated such a great wave of evil that I could not stride past it. Nor, for the entire world, would I have touched the thing. A red fire seemed to burn in its glass eyes as if it harbored a demon from Hell inside its stuffing. I whirled and someone grasped me by the collar. I found myself pushed into a dark corner, held prisoner by the drunken peasant, who bared his teeth and gnashed them in my face.

"Where?" he demanded. "Where is final page? We need it for Legion!"

I found I could not struggle. His eyes---my God, those horrible eyes!---held me prisoner more effectively than any bonds could have done. I could only babble, slobbering out my innocence, for I truly had no understanding of his question. He shook me, and banged my head against the wall, but got no more sensible answer. Then he grabbed my face in one filthy paw and looked directly into my soul. I knew that he was reading my mind, and no matter how I tried to close my thoughts, my entire life was as an open book to him. This is what you must understand, Mr. Holmes, and take precautions against, for he knows of your involvement, your interest in this case. I saw a fiend's smile creep onto his face, and blood pooled onto his bottom lip, where he had bitten it in his frenzy to torture me.

"So Sherlock Holmes is wizard. My master smell one. We burn house, but maybe he live."

I tried to struggle, to shake my head and deny it all. But such was pointless. The man---a brute, a beast, so much stronger than his size implied---hurled me to the floor and kicked me hard with his clumsy worker's boot. My friends finally rallied to my rescue, but by the time they reached me Mr. E was gone. I gestured wildly toward the door, but the doll had vanished as well, though my companions swore on their mothers' graves that it had never been there at all.

Mr. Holmes, I beg you, should you encounter us in the Shadows, do not speak of these things to my beloved wife. I am shamed for having gone on one last frolic, for betraying her in my thoughts and deeds. But I am also appalled to have been a pawn in a darker game, and to possibly have put your life in danger. Take care and heed my warning; avoid the peasant and his fiendish plaything."

By the time I read the last line, Holmes's head was sunk on his breast. "Why did they wait to kill him?" I asked. "They could have done away with him in the pub, and you would have had no warning."

"These are crafty foes," Holmes said, with infuriating calmness. "Our peasant---or should we call him the Russian Count, or the medical student?---knew of Smythe's plans to marry when he read his mind. How much easier to stage an accident on that day than to risk a fight in a tavern, where the villain's strength might be countered by the victim's numbers?"

I glanced down at the letter. "You spoke of avoiding a trap. Did you anticipate this as well?"

My friend shook his head. "Had I any suspicion that Smythe was truly endangered I would have seen that he was restrained within the Shadows. No, Watson, when I spoke of avoiding a trap, it was to stay away from the address Dr. Bradley submitted. If it is truly the residence of our foes, it will hardly be unguarded. Most likely it will be filled with snares, both physical and magical. If there is to be any trap, I shall set it."

I was gratified to hear my friend speak of action. "How will you do it?"

"With your help, of course. Will you aid me, Watson?"

I felt a renewed surge of pride and gratitude. "Of course, Holmes. What do you need me to do?"

He smiled thinly. "I need you to die."

Chapter Nineteen

"It is clear to me now," Holmes said, as he moved rapidly to set up his chemical apparatus. "I finally see our enemy's object, and his *modus operandi*."

"I would appreciate it if you would explain what you mean," I said, pausing in the act of unbuttoning a shirtsleeve. "It seems the least you could do, before you sacrifice me to the cause."

Holmes never looked up from his work. "Gilles de Rais arrived in this world at a wizard's summons, but he could not remain in this world without an anchor for his soul. Wraiths are, by their nature, fragile things. Possession of a willing host is possible, but it strains both parties. Therefore, our deceased wizard chose to become a *liche*---unable to totally reanimate a body, he hides inside an enchanted object, which acts as a repository for his soul. This object is properly known as a *phylactery*. If the phylactery is destroyed before the liche can find a permanent home, then the wraith can be driven back to the pits of Hell from which he was summoned."

"And the doll is his receptacle?"

Holmes nodded as he poured thick liquids together into a beaker, ignoring the ominous blue cloud their combination created at the mouth the glass. "Indeed, and Smythe's observations confirmed its unholy nature. The Russian keeps it by his side because the wraith directs him from within. No doubt the wraith once possessed the Russian, and now the two are connected so intimately that the Russian can speak languages he does not understand. But the wraith would prefer a real body, to taste evil pleasures once more." Holmes swirled the liquid, which had turned as luminous green as the froth that once dripped from the muzzle of the Baskerville hound. "Our Russian friend may be unaware that, as soon as Gilles de Rais attaches himself permanently to a body, his assistance will be both unnecessary and unwelcome. Surely the moment the French wizard is his own man, so to speak, he will murder his lackey. Perhaps by destroying the phylactery we can send one soul back to Hell and spare another from its torments, at least for a time."

"That is our goal, then? To find and smash this horrible doll?"

Holmes nodded. "We know the Russian purchases bodies. We know his master has failed once again in his efforts to permanently reanimate a corpse. Therefore they will require another body, very soon. We will offer them one, hopefully before Gilles de Rais can use his mesmerist to force another unfortunate gentleman to commit suicide."

I swallowed tightly. "And I will be that body."

Holmes held out the glass, where the fluid had now turned a strange shade of red. "Surely you remember your Shakespeare, Doctor? The potion that the friar gave Juliet, which so marvelously feigned death that she was laid to rest in her family's crypt? It is not such a difficult compound to concoct."

"What I recall is that her story had a rather tragic ending!"

"I could put a spell on you," Holmes continued, as if he had not taken my point. "But you must wear the hamsa for your own safely. It negates my magic and his."

"It would hardly negate a gun, or a rope, or even a strong pair of human hands!" I countered.

Holmes glanced my way just before adding a droplet of what looked like black tar to his mixture. "It will not come to that, Watson. You have my word, as both a professional and a friend."

He opened a drawer and removed his neat Moroccan case. Carefully, the familiar syringe, which had once been the grail of his addiction to cocaine, was now filled up with his noxious potion.

"There is no magic in this, Watson," he assured me. "Merely science. It will reduce you to a state of relaxation so deep you will be unable to speak or move, but you will be aware of your surroundings and all actions around you. The moment our task is complete, I will revive you. The antidote is surprisingly simple," he added, removing a flask from his pocket and waving it merrily.

"And if something interferes and you can not revive me?" I asked, wondering if I truly wished to hear his answer.

"The dose will dissipate naturally in about ten hours. You have my permission to indulge in a long winter's nap." He considered me for a moment. One eyebrow was raised, as if he had just noted my concerns about his plan. "Are you sincere in your offer, Watson? I would not wish to compel you against your will."

"I am always happy to assist you," I muttered, unable to conjure a level of enthusiasm equal to his. I held out my arm, but he shook his head.

"Not until we reach the mortuary."

With those chilling words, Holmes rose and reached for his coat. Within an hour, we were once again at the Dorset Street abode of the dead. Dr. Bradley was still in his pitiful office, slumped over an empty bottle and the remains of a squalid meal. Holmes slipped a note and substantial coinage to the assistant, who for once showed energy, tipping his hat and eagerly setting off on a journey to deliver a message to Bradley's special client.

"Watson, if you will?"

I steadied my nerve, calling on all the courage I had found when facing screaming Ghazis. Removing my coat and jacket, and loosening my shirtsleeves, I stretched myself atop the autopsy table. The flickering lamplight made the stacked coffins seem even more ominous. I was uncomfortably aware that in a corner of the room a genuinely dead body, that a young woman, rested beneath a stained cotton sheet. Moments passed, and then I heard footsteps. I was shocked to look up and find Bradley holding the syringe.

"A necessary deception," Holmes said, with a quick wink and a flourish of a hand over his face and disordered hair. "Not magical, I promise."

I nodded my acceptance and he plunged the needle into a vein. In mere heartbeats, I felt my body relax. I seemed to spiral, as if falling, the way one feels when at last dropping into an exhausted sleep. But I did not lose consciousness. Instead, I seemed to gain a perception outside of myself, as if floating free of my body, becoming a spirit able to hover inside the room. It was a sensation that was far from pleasant, especially as I found myself unable to communicate in any way with Holmes, yet able to stare down at my own form, which had taken on the distinctive discolorations of death.

There was a pounding at the door. Holmes removed a bottle from the apron he wore, splashing gin across his hands and face to add to the illusion of the drunken physician. I heard the groaning of the portal being opened, and then footsteps as they approached.

"He has no kin?"

The voice was thick and foreign. Removed from my own body, I watched as if I were a spectator at a play, seated high in the balcony. The Russian was nearly as tall as Holmes, clad in a black cape and wearing a battered hat that was some twenty years out of fashion. Thick, smoke-tinted spectacles covered his eyes, a startling contrast to the bone-whiteness of his skin. There was some show of beard, but thin and patchy. He was much younger than I had expected.

"None," Holmes said, with the air of a man who wants a thing done quickly, with few questions asked. "Toppled down the stairs and broke his neck, clumsy blighter."

"Then not suicide?"

"What the devil does it matter? He's dead and nobody will claim him."

"This different. I must ask," the Russian said. He reached into his cloak and removed the doll, placing it on the table beside me.

Had I possessed any strength or any control of my body, I surely would have given the game away at that instant, for the thing he settled within inches of my face radiated a fierce evil. The very innocence of its nature made it even more grotesque. The Russian bowed slightly, his hands folded like a worshipper before a shrine. His lips moved in silent prayer.

Inside myself, bound in my soul, I screamed.

At that second, Holmes sprang forward, wielding a scalpel. It changed in midair, growing in a flicker of reality to become a sword with fiery edges. It smashed down into the doll's porcelain head, shattering it into a thousand shards that flew everywhere around the room.

The Russian fell back, jabbering wildly in his own language.

We had won. Holmes had conquered. The Russian was on his knees, screeching and holding his hands over his ears. Holmes turned and looked to me, whispering a word of reassurance.

And then, from my impossible perch high above my body, I saw a black swarm begin to issue from the broken doll. Small, indistinct, insect-like, a horde of creatures whirled up from the object, spilling out and over, covering the table, the floor, and even my motionless body with a filthy, hellish tide. In an instant, they attacked Holmes, flooding over him in what looked like a seething liquid of their own nightmarish forms. I saw him throw out a hand, the light of magic rising from it, only to be instantly snuffed out by the sheer weight and impossible numbers of his unearthly assailants.

And then the blackness swallowed me completely.

Chapter Twenty

"Your friend Sherlock Holmes is a fool."

I looked to my companion. Since our misadventure in the Dorset Street mortuary, I could only estimate that three or four days had passed, based on the rough condition of my chin and the soiled state of my clothing. My captors had not allowed me to shave or bathe, and I had little sense of where we were going or how we were travelling, for I had been regularly rendered unconscious by generous applications of ether. Only a few moments before I had awoken on an uncomfortable bed, in a room whose wretched amenities---a chipped washbasin, a cracked mirror, and a tattered rug---suggested a cheap continental hotel. The room's single shutter was bolted, yet it was broken in enough places to admit light, as well as salty air that suggested an ocean was close by. In a half stupor, my head still pounding from the effects of the drug, I had attempted an investigation, and after some scratching about on the floor I discovered a yellowed copy of a newspaper. My Italian has never been fluent beyond ordering in a restaurant, yet I could tease out enough words to deduce my location.

Palermo. The place where the dead whispered.

And now I was facing my captor. I had caught glimpses of this individual so fleetingly that I half suspected they were figments of imagination, the wisps of a dream. She was perhaps thirty, with long brown hair already streaked with gray and a nose that had been broken and badly healed. She was dressed in a cheap ensemble so mismatched with checkered skirts and a stripped bodice that I wondered if she was ashamed to wear it in the streets. I settled at the room's small table, considering the meager offering of bread and soup that had been placed before me.

"Eat," she said. Her English was clear but oddly accented. "You will need your strength."

"You're going to kill me," I answered, shocked at how rough and weathered my voice emerged. My throat felt like it had been raked with vicious blades.

The woman shrugged. "Eventually. But not now."

I stared down at the food. Famished as I was, it appeared a feast, but my resolve was stronger.

"I will not dine with the witch who murdered my friend."

"Sherlock Holmes is not dead," the woman said. "Why would I kill the man who can obtain the missing page of the Devil's Bible and the spell that I came all the way from Hell to claim?"

I stared at her uncomprehendingly. She settled in the chair opposite me and pushed the bowl and a glass of wine closer.

"You do not recognize me, but perhaps my name is familiar. I am Gilles de Rais."

"How?" I said, even as my hand betrayed my resolve and reached for sustenance. "Gilles de Rais was a man!"

"Would you like to know the story, Doctor? Would you like to hear the truth before we proceed with our shared adventure?" Her dirty fingers glided toward me. I snatched away, and my lack of nourishment nearly claimed my consciousness. She chuckled and curled in her chair.

"Has the companion of the brilliant detective not yet guessed why Etienne Lellouche brought me from the pit? It was such an obvious thing. Etienne was my blood, my descendant. He thought that if he freed me I would help him become the most powerful sorcerer in the world. He believed that with my assistance he could conquer all of humanity with his magic. My deluded scion aimed pathetically low."

The woman---could this really be the fierce wizard of history, or was I still being deceived for some malevolent purpose?---motioned toward the corner of the room. The Russian emerged from the shadows and quickly poured more wine from a dark bottle.

"I should thank Etienne for the gift of Grigori, however. Etienne found my devoted servant in Siberia, while searching for arcane texts amid the ancient monasteries. He knew Grigori possessed the Shadowblood and lured him to England with promises of wealth and power. Grigori, as you know, can read minds."

160

I suddenly realized how utterly helpless I was. They knew everything about me, and about Holmes, for Grigori had searched my memories. If Smythe had been unable to resist him while conscious how much more had the Russian gained from me in my drugged and vulnerable state? They knew all, including the location of the last spell. My only consolation was that the Lady Hypatia's guardianship of that page would not falter, even if we had failed.

"I possessed the mind and body of Etienne, but only for a moment," the woman continued. "He welcomed me within, and in that instant I knew the limited scope of his ambition. And so I fled from him, into the bosom of Grigori. I linked our souls and our minds, so that we might share our thoughts and speak each other's language. My English was rusty at first, having not heard it since the war I fought beside the Maid of Orleans, but it soon improved."

"And the people at Urian Hall?" I asked.

"Easily dispensed with. They were dabblers, neophytes, and an embarrassment to the dark arts. I burned away Etienne's brain as I departed, and the others were quickly subdued. The fire covered our tracks."

I gnawed on the stale piece of bread. Perhaps if I could keep her talking, I could learn something that would help me. "Why didn't you stay inside of Grigori? Why enter the doll?"

"Possession it is an uncomfortable intimacy, Doctor. Grigori has lusts and perversions that I find appalling." She laughed. "And inside the phylactery my magic could grow again, become stronger. I could see and hear, I could give Grigori orders through our linked minds, but I could not *feel*." The woman threw her head back, groaning in a disgusting manner. "How much I long to feel!"

My hand shook as I grabbed the bowl of soup. "You murdered Thomas Gregson."

She looked back to me, yellow eyes filled with annoyance. "Of course I did. Grigori knew that Etienne had failed to gain the pages of the Devil's Bible, pages that Etienne had planned to present to me as an offering. It was essential that I have them---I had sought them even in my mortal lifetime. And so we went to the shop and Grigori used his eyes to order Gregson to give us the pages. But something went wrong. The timid little man did not fall under Grigori's sway as he should have, and we were forced to return later and steal what we needed."

He was almost blind, I thought. *And that protected him. He was terrified, but not overwhelmed.*

"When I realized that the page I most desired was missing from the collection, I was furious. I had Grigori find Gregson on Tower Bridge, and with a more concentrated force of his will he killed that miserable little bookman. But my rage was not quenched, and with every failed experiment it grew hotter. We returned to the shop, thinking perhaps we might find another binding spell within the ancient books. But as we approached that night I smelled your friend. Another wizard, a Shadowborn! I slipped into Grigori's body long enough to unleash Hellfire. I thought I had killed the interloper."

I found a bit of my spirit. "I am so sorry you were disappointed."

She glared at me and then burst into laughter. Twisting one hand into a fist, she leaned across the table and gave me a mock punch to my shoulder, as if I were her old regimental mate. "I like you, Doctor. You have a strong will. You would have made a great soldier in the army of Henry V, your country's Warrior King." She waved distractedly at an insect that had begun buzzing around our table, greedy for the crumbs of the wretched meal I had consumed. "I admire spirit in any man. I will reward you with more honesty---you may ask me what you will."

"Why are you a woman?"

She smirked at the directness of my question. "Our souls are neither male nor female, Doctor. Did you know that? I will confess my own ignorance. For too long I sought to reclaim a suit of skin that matched my former appearance. Etienne's spellbooks had burned in his mansion, but we had a reanimation spell from the pages of the Devil's Bible that we stole from Gregson's shop. It was a grand incantation, penned by the Archfiend himself, giving a method of permanently binding a wraith to a corpse. We chose young male specimens in the streets and pubs of Whitechapel. Grigori convinced them to kill themselves, and we retrieved them from the mortuary. Three times I was bound to a man's corpse, holding myself within it for hours. But then the spell failed, and I was forced to retreat into the doll."

Gilles de Rais leaned back, her shoulders quivering as she worked to suppress a sudden fit of giggling. "I do not see where murder is amusing," I said coldly.

"I only laugh because it was Sherlock Holmes who showed me the way to become mortal again."

"I do not believe you."

"Allow me to explain---we read the mind of the messenger you sent to lure us to the mortuary. It was our normal precaution, because we were wary of such magical traps, especially after Grigori pierced the mind of that fool Smythe. What if Holmes had been the wizard I sensed in the shop, and what if he had by some miracle survived the shop's burning? If so, would he not be in pursuit of us? A good general prepares his troops for any contingency.

"Grigori saw in the lackey's mind that it was Holmes, not Bradley, who waited for us at the mortuary. We came prepared for battle. When Holmes destroyed the phylactery in which my soul resided, scattering my dark magic, bits of it fell upon the only truly dead body in the morgue. It was the corpse of a prostitute, but I knew,

164

the instant a single fiber of my soul touched it, that it could hold me! Your friend had woefully underestimated my strength, and once Holmes was subdued, Grigori chanted the reanimation spell. As I drew breath inside this female form I understood the error of all our previous attempts. A single word of the incantation had been mistranslated by the wretched demon that wrote the spell! So now you understand my amusement."

"What did you do to Holmes?" I snapped.

"No permanent damage, I assure you. Grigori attempted to read his mind, but made no progress, so we pierced yours instead, and learned the truth of the spell's location. Before we departed we left Holmes a message, scrawled in blood across the wall of the mortuary. He has one week to join us here in Palermo, with the missing page of the Devil's Bible in hand. He will do this, Dr. Watson, or we will send you straight to Hell."

"You can kill me," I said, watching as the tiny insect perched on the rim of my wine glass. I knew the little creature; I had recognized the dusting of gold about its wings. It gave me a surge of courage to see Holmes's familiar so close to my side. "I do not fear you, Gilles de Rais, for you cannot touch my soul."

"Have you not been without a soul before, Doctor? You deceive yourself if you think I lack such power. I may have been born a mortal man, and reborn a mortal woman, but my grasp of the darkness is stronger than it has ever been."

I recalled the hamsa. Instinctively, my hand flew to my throat. My captors both laughed loudly. The glittering bee took flight.

"It would be an irresponsible wizard indeed who did not ward his mortal companions," Gilles de Rais said. "I sensed it on you the moment I was whole again. Luckily, it was simple enough to force the real Dr. Bradley to remove it for us, so that we could leave it as a souvenir for your friend. We killed the physician afterward, of course, but from his sorry state I would say he is no great loss to this world."

With that announcement, she held up her hand, palm open. For a moment, I thought I saw an image there, an outline of the hamsa. Just as I saw it, it began to burn.

"Sherlock Holmes now has a scar he can not remove, nor cover with a glamour. A trophy to tell him how miserably he has failed."

Chapter Twenty-one

I roared with rage, and in a burst of energy I shot to my feet and flipped the table. Gilles de Rais toppled in a flurry of skirts. Grigori charged forward, massive fists clenched, no doubt intending to crush my skull like an eggshell. I stepped into his assault, slamming my shoulder into his chest. I heard him give a startled cry, and had the satisfaction of hearing the air whoosh from his lungs. He fell like a massive oak, and I leapt over him, seizing the sole candle that sputtered on the room's only shelf. I hurled it at the woman, gratified to see it catch in her dress and erupt in greasy burst of orange flame. To the sound of her screams, I raced to the door. It was locked, but with a determined, desperate speed I kicked it down. I dared not look backwards, but ran through the debris to the landing of the outer stairs.

And then I halted, skidding to a stop, arms flailing as I reclaimed my balance. I slammed back against the wall, gasping for breath.

Before me was not a single staircase, but a dozen, descending and twisting at impossible angles, some stable, others moving slowly, and even more of them writhing violently like agitated snakes. I could see people walking, climbing, and dancing on the stairs: some upside down, others at ninety-degree angles. The motion made me dizzy. It took all my resolve not to faint, or be sick upon my shoes.

"This is an illusion," I hissed. I had not been Sherlock Holmes's companion in the Shadows for nothing. "It is not real."

"True," the sultry voice of Gilles de Rais answered. Suddenly she was at my side, half her hair burnt away, the smoldering tatters of her dress clutched to her nearly naked body. "But what is reality? Are you standing on the threshold of a street, or on the outer stairs, some five stories above the piazza? If you move forward, will you gain your freedom or plunge to your death? If you choose incorrectly, even your celebrated wizard friend cannot save you."

"No," I heard myself say, and once again I felt that strange sensation, that I was leaving my body, freeing my soul. "But maybe my death can save him."

And with that I plunged forward, falling into the twirling skeleton of stairways, plunging ever downward until once again I met with blackness.

**

I awoke in the land of the dead.

Slowly, I sat up, shocked that I was still alive. I found myself in a long, narrow, frigid room filled with mummified remains. The light was timid and flickering, as if provided by invisible candles. Everywhere I looked, the forms of long dead monks hung on the walls, each one bearing a placard around his neck. All were clad in the habits of the Capuchins. Some were little more than skeletons, while others retained enough flesh to hint at what they had been in life: a fat man, one with strangely red hair, another with a ponderous mole on his cheek. I twisted, and on the opposite wall I saw shallow niches filled with supine figures clad in more secular attire. Some wore boots and spurs, while others clutched rusted swords. I saw insignia that indicated generals and captains, yet above them and to the rear of the room was an even more remarkable sight, an archway filled with the bodies of young women, all clad in white gowns, with withered wreaths of flowers upon their heads.

A memory came back to me. I recalled pictures I had seen on a continental tour and stories I had heard from other friends about the mysteries of the great catacombs of Palermo.

I climbed to my feet and took a few steps forward, seeking a better view of the remains. Abruptly, I felt a violent restraint to my ankle and heard an ominous rattle and creaking. Twisting around, I saw that the metal racks of dead monks just above me were shivering, as if something had disturbed their eternal rest.

"Take care, Doctor." It was the voice of Gilles de Rais, radiating and echoing from all corners of the room. I could barely separate the words, as they seemed to swirl and crash back upon each other. "If you will look down, you will find that you are chained to the trellis that supports our dearly departed brethren. Unless you wish to be crushed and impaled by their bones, I would suggest you make no effort to escape."

"Why here?" I demanded. "Saint Rita knew you were coming here---but why?"

"To raise the Legion of the Damned, of course," the voice answered. I turned a tight circle. Gilles de Rais was still hidden, but at last I located Grigori, standing in the shadows near a pillar. Above him, more rows of the dead dangled from long metal spikes like macabre ornaments on an evil tree. "Surely you do not think that all the corpses in a church are holy? The sinners here are numerous and easily stirred. And they have been eagerly waiting for us, waiting to be freed. Once we have the spell for creating the Legion of the Damned, nothing can stop us from bringing them back, resurrecting them once again as warriors for my cause."

"You seek revenge on God," I said, still looking all around for the source of her words.

"I have no quarrel with God," the voice sneered. "My fight is with Satan, who betrayed me, who abandoned me to my death and then mocked me and tortured me for centuries! I have no interest in Heaven, but once my army is formed, I have all intentions of marching on Hell!"

I recalled Holmes's words, about the lines of power, how this very place was a crossroads where boundaries were weakened.

"And if the earth is torn apart by such a war?" I asked, imagining the horror of a battle between wraiths and demons, with the fighting spilling out, encompassing the poor people in the city. Palermo would be destroyed. The supernatural war would spread and no mortal could stop it. I could not grasp where, or if, it would end.

I felt a breath on my neck. I whirled, jerking on the chain. Above me, the vast array of bodies swayed and began to fall. I gave a cry and covered my head, a pitiful, final action.

The terrible descent abruptly ceased; the bodies swung in midair. Slowly, they shifted back, as the great metal platform they hung from righted itself against the wall.

Gilles de Rais stood next to me, holding out one arm. She had exchanged her burnt dress for a peasant's blouse and trousers much too big for her frame, with sandals upon her feet. Most of her hair was gone, and I took some satisfaction in seeing that she was either unable to heal herself or unwilling to divert what magical resources her spirit possessed. Half her face was covered in blisters, and her left eye had turned completely white.

"I care nothing for the world and its fate, though perhaps indulging my whims with a few children would not be amiss. Despite my new form I still have certain...*appetites*," she hissed. She lifted a hand to stroke my face, and with a predator's smile, she retreated. I twisted and played the only card that remained.

"Grigori!" I shouted to the Russian. "Do not be deceived! She is going to kill you! She has no need of you now---you are nothing to Gilles de Rais! Flee while you can!"

The woman laughed. "Save your breath. You see, our friend Grigori can only speak and understand English if I permit him to do so through the link in our minds. Otherwise, Grigori recognizes only his native tongue. Tell me, Doctor, do you speak Russian?"

All was lost. I turned and sought the courage to meet my end with dignity. "Very well, Madame. But I will save you time...feel free to kill me now."

There was an ancient altar some twenty feet away, with a high backed chair beside it. Gilles de Rais took the seat, placing her chin upon her folded hands. "So eager to die, Doctor? I thought you were a fiercer man than that."

"I am merely being courteous, Madame. Sherlock Holmes will not give you the spell you seek. He will not unleash your evil plans."

"Even to save your life?"

"What is one man's life to the world?" I found I could force a smile. "My friend's mathematical powers are phenomenal, and that is a simple equation." I took a deep breath, readying myself for whatever method of execution the fiend would select. "And even if he chose my life over all of humanity's, he does not have the page you seek, nor will the guardian of the Library of the Arcane give it to him. He cannot take it from the Lady Hypatia."

"Watson," a dry voice proclaimed, echoing in the chamber, "you have a distressing lack of faith in my powers."

Chapter Twenty-two

A burst of light and heat knocked me to the ground. Above me, the mummies rattled and danced in their chains. Gilles de Rais rose from her perch, and Grigori stalked forward, a pistol in each hand.

Between us was the figure of Sherlock Holmes. He held the Lady Hypatia against his side, and before any of us could speak or react he flung her to the ground with a savagery that was alien to his nature. I crawled the full distance my bond would allow, and saw that her face was slack and unconscious, her long hair a mass of tangles.

I looked to my friend. His eyes had changed, had turned black and flat. His voice was icy and virtually unrecognizable as he spoke.

"Gilles de Rais, permit me to introduce the Lady Hypatia, guardian of the spell of the Legion of the Damned. She did not come to this interview willingly, I assure you."

"Impressive," Gilles de Rais said, with a mocking round of applause. "But any conjurer of Charles VII's court could have done the same. I am hardly impressed with spectacular entrances. I find they usually lead to disappointing exits."

Her left hand snapped out, and suddenly my ankle burned as if it had been thrust into a steamer's boiler. I grabbed at the chain, only to find it tightened at my touch. Just as I screamed with the pain, the burning ceased, and I was left whimpering in its wake.

"I trust that is demonstration enough for you, Mr. Holmes? Any further attempt at magic and your friend dies."

"There is no need for further exhibitions," Holmes said. "I believe we can reach an agreement. I have the page you seek."

"Truly? Then why did you bother to bring her?" Gilles de Rais asked, pointing to the unconscious Lady. "What is your game?"

"There is no game," Holmes said. "I present her to you as a gift and as proof of my sincerity. She is immortal, so if you desire you may torture her in any method that you please, for as long as you like."

Holmes gave a slight bow as he said this. The action caused a tight fist to seize in my stomach. Gilles de Rais scowled.

"I do not believe it is so simple. You value Dr. Watson, if not this woman."

One dark brow lifted. "Perhaps we do not yet understand each other," Holmes said. "I value Watson not at all."

My heart froze at those words. Holmes looked to me, and I saw a stranger. Yet something rang true in his tone and his stance, as much as I shook my head and stammered a denial of his words. He had changed. I understood it now, that he had become a different man. A transformation had been occurring in the days since our return from America. He had used me cruelly, had put my life in peril multiple times. He had killed me, in essence, without a second thought.

The Lady Hypatia showed no signs of reviving. What had Holmes done to her?

"But Grigori has looked inside the doctor's mind," Gilles de Rais sneered. "You are his friend, his hero!"

Sherlock Holmes calmly folded his arms. "And surely your creature has also seen that John Watson is a very *stupid* man."

As silently as I could, I gathered the Lady Hypatia up and dragged her back into the shadows below the wall of mummies. Gilles de Rais stepped away from her throne and gave Holmes a cool appraisal.

"You have piqued my interest, sir. Why are you now so cold to your companions and generous to me?"

I looked down and began gently stroking the Lady's face. There was a deep wound upon her temple. Blood was clotted in her hair. I had seen her restored before, but to my horror, she now gave no sign of awakening. I lifted my eyes, seeking some comfort, an image of a merciful deity to receive my prayers.

Behind us, high in a balcony chamber, something moved. I caught only a flicker of it, and was unsure of what I had seen, whether it was friend or foe or merely a trick of the unnatural light.

"Because our interests are aligned," Holmes said to Gilles de Rais, as calmly as he might discuss the results of a case over a fine repast at *Simpson's*. "I am proposing an alliance between us, wizard to wizard. Together, we can defeat the Devil at his own game. We can command the Legion of the Damned to storm Satan's castle, we can use the Fiend's own magic against him. And once we are done, we can divide all the planes of existence between us. You can rule the world of Sun and I will take the Shadows."

It was more than I could bear, especially as I saw Holmes reach into his great travelling cape and produce a familiar document.

"No! Holmes, stop, this is madness!"

"Watson, I will thank you to hold your foolish tongue!" he snapped. His eyes had once again changed. Now they glowed with red flames, bright enough that even Gilles de Rais took a step backward from him. "This is your doing, Watson. You and that woman, who called me back to the Shadows when I had renounced them. See what you have brought about!"

Gilles de Rais began to smile. She spoke again, an order in Russian. Grigori stowed one pistol in his belt. He took the page from Holmes and made a show of presenting it to his mistress, then turned and leveled the remaining gun at Holmes while the woman read the document.

"Lovely," she purred. "With all the proper elements." She laughed, as if finding an unexpected ingredient in a familiar recipe. "But I see that Shadowblood is required."

"Indeed," Holmes said. "I knew it the moment I first read the spell, deep in the vaults of the Library of the Arcane. Without my aid, you <u>cannot</u> raise your Legion."

I started to shout, to make another objection, however impotent it might be, but the slightest pressure on my right hand stopped me. I looked down and saw that the Lady's eyelids had begun to flutter even as the terrible wound was starting to heal.

Holmes held out his right arm, his free hand shoving back his cuff. Gilles de Rais produced a knife, taking his hand and turning his wrist.

"Should I mistrust you?" she asked.

"No, for curiosity is my besetting sin, Madame. And I have never seen a Legion of the Damned."

She sliced the knife across his wrist. Blood spilled down, a long, thin thread of crimson that pooled in the stones beneath his feet. Grigori seemed enticed by it, kneeling to examine the offering, which even as we watched was separating magically into a dozen or more tentacles of fluid. The blood whisked out across the floor as Gilles de Rais chanted strange words from the page. I saw the dark lines crawl the walls, shoot into the stones, and embrace the dozens of corpses that hung in the niches and on the racks. The blood became threads, spinning around them, forming thick cocoons. Each nest and web then began to pulsate, like the beating of a massive heart.

Grigori gibbered, clapping his hands and squatting at the puddle of enchanted blood. His antics interrupted the spell, a crass counterpoint to the crescendo of magic. Gilles de Rais dropped her head. Sweat drizzled down her face, which had grown grey and leaden. Whatever enchantment she had worked had tired her. I recalled Holmes's words about the limitations of mortal magicians.

But Holmes was half mortal as well. As I watched, even more blood coursed down from his arm. The wound continued to flow freely. It was surely enough to weaken any man, not matter what Shadow ancestry he claimed. I saw my friend sway slightly and blink his eyes rapidly, as if willing himself to remain conscious.

Gilles de Rais glanced at her wayward companion, whose behavior was growing ever more repulsive and obscene. Clearly, the sight of blood aroused him, the way a beautiful woman's portrait might entice a normal man.

"He is tiresome," Gilles de Rais said.

"Then kill him," Sherlock Holmes softly suggested.

A word was spoken. Grigori launched into the air. He slammed against the pillar behind him, and with a ripping sound a metal spear that held a corpse pierced his chest, impaling him some twenty feet above our heads. His face fell back, his expression one of shock, agony, and betrayal. His arms and legs twitched several times, blood bubbled from his lips. Then, with a final groan, he was still.

"Our work is done," Gilles de Rais whispered. "And it is time for my Legion to fight."

She flung out her hands, shoving my friend backwards. Holmes fell, splashing in the bloody pool. All around us, the scarlet cocoons ripped open. Down from the niches and the walls came newly-restored bodies in the forms of monks and knights and soldiers. Even the women in white dresses dropped to the floor, shrieking and baring their teeth. The legion shouted battle cries in half a dozen languages. They beat upon weapons and stamped their feet, until the din was nearly deafening and the entire room seemed to shake. I could imagine the entire catacomb collapsing, burying us all.

Only the feel of the Lady Hypatia clinging to me, having come back to life in my arms, gave me any hope. Holmes was unconscious.

"By the old gods," the Lady Hypatia murmured. "What is happening? *What has he done*?!"

"Now we will storm Hell!" Gilles de Rais shrieked, over the swelling noise. "Rally to me and we will kill the father of lies!" As I watched, the dead began to form ranks behind her, like obedient soldiers. Gilles de Rais raised a hand with a curled fist, as confident in her military bearing as her mortal predecessor had been in his. With her other hand, she pointed to Holmes.

"This man thought he would share my power. He wanted to divide the worlds between us. He thinks he is my equal in magic!"

The wraiths howled. Their bloodlust was electric, and a static heat prickled across my skin. The Lady Hypatia gave a single sob and buried her face in my chest.

"Clearly, he was wrong," Gilles de Rais laughed. "I will use his skin for my banner when I march into Perdition. But first, there is one small matter..."

She pointed to when I crouched, with the Lady trembling against me.

"Kill them!" she said.

Chapter Twenty-three

One of the women strode forward. She had flaming red hair and she carried a short sword, the weapon of a Roman legionnaire. She was breathtaking in her loveliness; clearly she had been one of the legendary beauties ensconced in the Chamber of Virgins. She halted with her weapon raised, as if pondering whom she should slay first.

Then she spun and plunged her sword into Gilles de Rais's side.

"You bitch!" the red-haired woman screamed. "I knew Long Alice! She was as fine a whore as ever roamed the streets of Whitechapel! How dare you steal her body!"

Gilles de Rais staggered backward, clutching at the wound. Her face crumpled in confusion at this turn of events. "What? Who...who are you?"

"A better woman than you'll ever be!"

All around her, the army was now breaking apart, slipping out of rank and dropping weapons. Gilles de Rais staggered, then held out a hand and began shrieking magical commands. The words went unheeded. Indeed, the very soldiers she had raised from death now formed a circle and began to mock her, shouting taunts in very profane English. Some of their epithets were ripe enough to make a sailor blush.

"I do not understand---obey me! You must obey me!" Gilles de Rais shrieked. "I am your general, your leader!"

"No," Sherlock Holmes said. He was climbing to his feet, still swaying, his left hand staunching the wound on his wrist. "By the power given to me by their summoner, I am their commander. They were never yours."

Gilles de Rais stared. "The spell--"

"Rewritten," Holmes answered. His face had changed. His eyes were their normal grey, and all the odd darkness had fled. "As Watson can tell you, I am a skillful and cunning liar when it suits my purposes."

Gilles de Rais screamed in rage. She threw a bolt of power at my friend. To my horror, Holmes could not raise a defense in time. He toppled backward, but shouted an order, and at once every denizen of the crypt fell on the reborn magician. For an instant it seemed that they would tear her limb from limb. Then there was an explosion, and the legion was thrown skyward. I barely managed to cover my head and protect the Lady who was still half-fainting in my arms. Bodies flew all around me. I heard moans and curses; clearly even the newly reborn could feel mortal pain.

Gilles de Rais stood in the midst of a circle of green Hellfire. The air around her crackled and shot sparks. I understood enough of Holmes's ways to know that she was warding herself. She was now protected from all unnatural assaults, including those of the wraith army.

"You fool," she hissed Holmes. "Perhaps you win this round, but you will pay a heavy price. Watch him burn!"

Flames flared on the chain that bound me. I saw them creeping forward, link by link, glowing green.

"You cannot stop it," the ancient wizard in the woman's body called. "You cannot break or undo this spell. As long as my soul survives, Hellfire burns what it was tasked for! He dies and none of your Shadow magic can kill me."

It came then---the retort that I knew so well from my army days. It was the familiar snap of a rifle. At the same instant, a red flower bloomed in the exact middle of Gilles de Rais's forehead. It seemed to confuse her. Her lips moved soundlessly. Then she fell, dropping amid her own flames.

But the Hellfire on the chain did not go out, and now something was rising from the circle, something like a black cloud formed by a writhing mass of insects. Gilles de Rais had slipped the mortal body, but the evil wraith that was his soul lingered. I looked to Holmes, expecting him to use another enchantment, to rip the cursed being apart.

He did nothing. His head fell forward in defeat and shame.

The flame on the chain moved two links closer. I pushed the Lady Hypatia away to prevent her being incinerated at my demise. Holmes had failed and nothing could save me. The wraith howled as the last link ignited.

"No!" a strong voice called, ringing out from the darkness beneath the balcony. "Go back to Hell, where you belong."

A woman in a nun's habit and wimple stepped from the shadows. She gestured imperiously, like a mistress to a disobedient servant. The wraith twisted, cringing and shrieking. The nun gently pressed a bare foot to a spot in the cobblestone floor.

The ground opened at her touch. There was a burst of green light and a great sucking noise. My eyes felt scalded. The wraith fought and writhed, but it was quickly pulled down, disappearing through the newly created void. In an instant the room was silent, the floor was whole, and the flame on the chain was extinguished.

Saint Rita of Cascia, the Patroness of Impossible Causes, dusted off her hands.

There was a moment of uncertainty, when I felt that I might still topple over into an abyss of unconsciousness. Then something cool and soft touched my face. I looked down to find the Lady Hypatia smiling up at me.

"It is over," she whispered, and directed my attention to the place where Holmes now stood next to the beaming saint.

"True, at times my Shadow weapons are useless," Holmes said. "But on those occasions I find a Martini-Henry .45 caliber will serve nicely." He turned and signaled to the balcony. "We are all fortunate that Tobias Gregson is such an excellent marksman."

"Who...who are these people?" I asked, as Holmes knelt and whispered a word that broke the manacle from my leg. Though some were still shaking their heads or muttering profanities, none of the resurrected company seemed to be seriously injured.

"Surely you recognize a few old friends, Doctor. I am sure that Mary Kelly remembers you."

The woman came forward, putting all the suggestiveness of the Whitechapel streets into her stride. "That I do. Nellie Gwyn here does as well!"

Several of the figures drew closer, and I could pick out the familiar faces of the Whitechapel sisterhood and the famous actors. Others were unknown to me, but all had lost the fierceness they projected when Gilles de Rais had raised them as the Legion of the Damned.

"So they are not lost souls?"

"No, but merely friendly ghosts," Holmes said, offering his hand to help me to my feet. "I trust you are not hurt?"

"No," I asserted as I in turn assisted the Lady to rise. "How dare you think so!"

Surely Holmes sensed more than astonishment at the nature of our rescue. Perhaps he heard the anger I could not completely suppress. The Lady Hypatia stared at him before whispering something in Latin. With a burst of energy, she drew back her arm and slapped Holmes across the face. The assembled spirits roared in laughter.

"I deserved that," Holmes said, but without further explanation he turned to the ghosts. "I thank you all for your good work. Go in peace."

They began to fade as the bodies they had possessed and animated turned once again to mummies. Corpses and bones piled all around our feet. I wondered how the good Capuchin fathers would ever reassemble them. Only the five women of Whitechapel hesitated. The tallest shook her fist at Holmes.

"You will remember your promise. A deal was made, and signed in blood! We will have justice."

"You shall," Holmes said.

They slid away into the ether just as Inspector Gregson appeared, resting his rifle on his shoulder. Holmes warmly shook his hand. The inspector's expression was troubled, but resolute.

"That was a close thing, Mr. Holmes, though you certainly predicted it, as well as any prophet could. I hope you will forgive me for not believing you from the start."

"The very existence of the Shadows is a hard thing to accept," Holmes said. "Watson will bear witness to that." He gestured toward the exit. "I was fortunate in that Professor Steele was willing to be an accomplice to our plot. Without her summoning so many restless spirits, we could never have arranged such a convincing deception."

Gregson made a wry smile. "I thought I would never get her up those stairs in time to save you. That wretched female must weigh as much as one of the Queen's carriage horses! She nearly had a seizure going up---perhaps Dr. Watson had better see to her health in coming down."

I nodded and was about to step forward when I noticed Saint Rita had slipped away from us. I saw her praying beside a crucifix on the wall. The Lady Hypatia was now berating Holmes in what sounded like a mixture of Greek and Aramaic. Hurriedly, I moved to the side of the incorruptible nun.

"I---Madame---Blessed One," I said, recalling Holmes's form of address. "You saved my life. How can I ever thank you?"

She whispered a final prayer and genuflected. As she looked up at me, she began to fade away, growing ever more indistinct.

"Take care of Mr. Holmes. A darkness gathers around him. He cannot fight it alone."

I was struggling to reply when a moan from above us froze us all in our tracks. We looked skyward. Grigori was conscious, struggling against the pike that held him, weakly pleading for help. Holmes considered the man through narrowed eyes.

"I fear you have a more critical patient, Doctor. That man has proved distressingly difficult to kill."

Chapter Twenty-four

"Brother Mycroft! This is certainly a surprise."

I swung my legs down from the sofa, wincing at a reminder of our fight in the crypts of Palermo. We had been in London less than a week, and I had spent most of that time recovering from my strange journey, eating and sleeping, occasionally lulled adrift by the sonorous melodies of Holmes's violin. I had also taken long walks in Regent's Park, and even a pointless train journey to Oxford and back, answering quite curtly in the negative when Holmes inquired if he should join me.

In truth, I was trying to escape the oppressive thoughts that had been mine ever since awakening in Palermo. Holmes was far too talented at reading my mind, even without the hypnotic powers that Grigori had possessed, and I did not wish him to know what pathways those thoughts were taking. Mycroft's arrival was, in truth, a welcome diversion from an inner debate that had been raging for days.

"What has brought you from your circuit?" Holmes asked. "And with a personal appearance at that, which is surely a sign of the apocalypse. Here, take the largest chair."

Mycroft---my friend's brother who excelled him not only in age and weight, but in supreme reasoning intelligence---settled his bulk into a seat with a grateful snort. In his usual manner, he dismissed all pleasantries and drove immediately to his point.

"That was a bad business in Palermo. Why in the name of the Shadows did you not consult me?"

"Because it was not your concern," Holmes said, with some testiness. "I saw no need to draw you into it."

"Ah, but as a result, you nearly had your friend Watson killed. Doctor," he said, with a wave of his flipper-like hand in my direction, "if you have any common sense at all, you will abandon my sibling. Surely the royalties from your stories will allow you to afford better rooms?"

Holmes folded his arms. "I trust you have come here for something more important than a tongue lashing or to inspire treason in the ranks!"

Mycroft was not deterred from his scolding. "And such mistreatment of the Lady Hypatia as well! Can you imagine how I felt when I received a note from her telling me that you had smashed her in the head! With no warning! Brother, you misogyny is legendary, but this is taking it too far."

"It was necessary," Holmes said coldly. I had heard the same explanation on the train from Palermo, and it rankled now as it had at the time. "Neither Watson nor the Lady are skilled dissemblers---forgive me my frankness, old friend, but you know it to be the truth. And she had taken a vow not to surrender the final page of the Devil's Bible. The only way to take it from her was to render her unconscious, and she is quite immune to chloroform."

I had not found the argument compelling, and neither had the Lady, who had refused to return to London with us. Holmes had travelled with her to Palermo via the Shadows, but she much preferred a private voyage home, in a first class cabin, at my friend's expense.

"It was inexcusable," Mycroft said.

"Necessary," Holmes repeated, in a voice like ice.

Mycroft pulled a cigar from his coat. Holmes did not seem inclined to be hospitable, so I provided a match.

"Thank you, Doctor. However, I did not come solely to chastise my naughty brother. I came because I have news that I felt would be best delivered in person. It is about the Russian. Do you know who he is?"

"Grigori is a quarter-blood," Holmes replied, "with enough Shadow magic in his veins to be dangerous. He has the potential to become a powerful wizard in his own right---any individual who can summon Hellfire, even if possessed by another at the time, is not to be dismissed. Moreover, his powers of mesmerism are vast and a threat to all who come in contact with him." Holmes settled in his own chair as I reclaimed the sofa. "He is currently confined in close quarters at Scotland Yard, in manacles with a black hood over his head. As an extra precaution, no one is to approach him without benefit of special goggles, which I have provided. They immediately neutralize the effects of his horrible eyes."

Mycroft shook his head. "I am sorry, Sherlock, but I am going to have to remove him from confinement and send him back to Russia."

Holmes and I exchanged baffled glances. "You cannot," my friend protested. "I have promised Inspector Gregson this man will hang for the murder of his brother!"

"Such promises are worthless in the face of the Great Game. Your suspect is a player, a pawn on the board. I must return him to his homeland."

Holmes gave a lion's roar. "You will not!"

Mycroft considered him coolly. "I will and there is nothing you can do about it."

"Explain yourself."

"You know my special gift. You know it is more powerful than your own." He blew out smoke in a long stream. For an instant, I seemed to see figures within the dark curtain it created. Men with guns raced forward, fell over barriers made of wire. More men on horses charged across desolate plains, and strange mechanized vehicles shot them down. "I see what is coming. It is a chill east wind that will blow the world apart. Your Grigori is part of it."

"No."

"Sherlock, this is not your decision to make. The pieces are in play. This Grigori was already considered a holy man in his small village in Siberia. Etienne Lellouche found him and brought him to London to assist the summoning, but it was Gilles de Rais who saw his powers and chose him as an apprentice. Yet all of this was but a diversion from his ultimate fate, which is tied to the undoing of the world."

"Then let us hang him," Holmes snarled. "And the wind will not blow, nor the world come apart."

Mycroft waved away the images, scattered the dead and dying. "That wind must blow. The world must change and magic must be banished from it. Our time is coming to an end, dear Brother. The Shadows will fade and vanish, and there is nothing you can do to stop it."

"I care nothing for the Shadows," Holmes said. Both hands clenched into fists. "I demand justice for Thomas Gregson!"

Mycroft shrugged. "What is one dead man to history? I am sorry, Sherlock. You would do better to wipe the slate clean. Tomorrow Grigori Rasputin will begin his journey home, accompanied by guards who are capable of resisting both his magic and yours. Good day, Brother."

Mycroft grunted with the effort of hoisting his bulk from the chair. Holmes wandered to the window. I attempted an awkward farewell, but Mycroft turned with his hand on the door.

"Sherlock, is it true that you made a bargain with the Bloody Five of Whitechapel?"

"I did," my friend said.

"That was...unwise," Mycroft rumbled. "I have said, when the time comes, I shall return to the Shadows. But you, dear Brother, must take care, lest you lose your very soul to something even darker."

**

"This is a night for breaking promises," Holmes said, nursing a glass of brandy. It had begun to rain and the evening was bitterly cold. Our small fire provided little protection against the rawness of London at her grimmest. "My brother gave me his word, many years ago, that he would never interfere in my work. As much as he found solving problems for mortals beneath his dignity, he would never intervene to prevent me from seeing justice done."

"Perhaps he had no choice."

"With Mycroft there is always a choice," Holmes sneered. "But because he is so gifted with the Sight he deludes himself otherwise."

"The Sight?"

"Precognition. My brother can see into the future. Not exact events, but great patterns, the shifting of historical tides."

"And he sees that a war is coming."

Holmes nodded. "While I do not share the strength of his gift, at times I have flashes of it. He is correct, there will be a war, unlike any the world has known. And it seems young Rasputin has a role to play in it. Would that I had killed him when I had the chance, or that Gilles de Rais had possessed better aim when she impaled him on that pike." Holmes drained his glass and walked to the mantel. After an instant he gave a hiss of anger and shattered the glass inside the fireplace. He turned with his hands clasped behind his back. "And now I must break my oath to you."

"How so?" I asked. I was already wary, but his words set me on edge.

"I swore an oath that I would never work my magic against humanity. Like a physician, I would do no harm. But tonight I must meet with Inspector Gregson and wipe away all memory of his actions in this affair. I will strip him of his heroism, his courage. I will implant new memories of tepid events and a long search for clues that had no results. In his mind, his brother's killer will remain at large, and he will never know the truth of the Shadows. You will be nothing but a faithful companion to me, the talented amateur detective."

"Will this be difficult?"

"Hardly. Such magic comes as easy to me as breathing. Watson, the potential for great evil lurks inside me." He leaned against the mantel. His posture reminded me of a man facing a firing squad. "I think you know this now, more deeply than you have ever known it before."

"You could have...*warned* me," I said, wishing I could shape my true feelings, the anger and frustration, into better words. "I would gladly fight beside you, against any enemy, if only the battle were clear to me from the start."

"I had hoped you would recognize my familiar."

"I did," I snapped. "But you, in that place..." I shook my head. "You have deceived me before, once when I thought you were dying and for three years when I believed you dead. You push things too far!"

Holmes accepted my outburst with a nod of surrender. "You would do well to heed my brother's advice. It would be in your best interests to leave me."

"Holmes-"

He extended his right hand, palm outward. It was then that I saw clearly what he had taken some pains to hide on our journey homeward from Palermo. There was indeed a scar on his palm, the impression of the hamsa that Gilles de Rais had burned into his flesh as a reminder of his failure to protect me.

"I am far from perfect, Watson. I am fallible, and I often take unacceptable risks. I do not deserve the loyalty and friendship that has been offered to me. The Blessed One, Saint Rita, saw it clearly. Perhaps that was what she was trying to warn me of all along."

I ducked my head, lest he see in my expression that for some time my thoughts had run in that very direction. His work was dangerous, and after this incident, I had found my trust in him shaken to the core. There was our long friendship, of course, but was it strong enough to survive?

"How did you convince a saint in Heaven to come to your aid?" I asked. Of all our defenders, she was the most unlikely. Holmes appeared startled. He favored me with that old expression which asked why I was so dull I had not figured this out for myself.

"I said your name. It was all that was required."

The clock ticked loudly. For a time I did not speak. At last, recalling the saint's final words to me, I took a deep breath.

"Do you wish me to stay?"

"How often have I said," Holmes answered softly, "that I would be lost without my Boswell? By lost I did not mean missing to history, or confused in my direction. I would be lost in a far greater and more important sense, for all eternity."

His words pressed on my conscience. I found that I had clenched my hands tightly. I forced them to relax.

"Then of course I will stay," I said.

Holmes considered me somberly. This moment seemed to stretch out, beyond the reality of our room, into some great and yet unknown future. Finally a smirk, almost childish in its twitching amusement, formed on my friend's face.

"Until the next marriage comes along, I presume? You would abandon me for a wife, I think. It is the only selfish aspect of your nature."

"Not every man is a cold and inhuman thinking machine, Holmes!"

"And let us be grateful for that, or humanity would soon cease to exist. And on that note, I have another favor to ask of you."

"I will not pretend to be a corpse again, no matter how you beg."

"Hardly that, Watson. Our friend Nevil Maskelyne was delighted to learn that the 'ghosts' of Professor Steele's show were no more than clever projections cast down by a new style of projector he was unable to find because it was concealed in the ceiling of the theater, rather than below the stage."

"What rot!" I exclaimed. Holmes waved aside my disgust.

"Falsehoods sometimes serve a good cause. And as Professor Steele has wisely decided to return to America, our magician friend is fully satisfied with this explanation. I would accept no payment for my small role in this matter, but the Great Maskelyne was good enough to send us two tickets to the opening night of his grand new production at the Egyptian Hall. You have no objection to sleight of hand, I presume? Or to pretty women being produced out of colored boxes and elephants disappearing in thin air?"

"None whatsoever," I chuckled.

"Excellent. Then hurry and put on your evening clothes. You may wish to take a late dinner afterward."

"But you are going to see Gregson tonight."

"Indeed I am. However, I was alerted this morning that the Lady Hypatia's ship had docked and she is once again in residence at the Library of the Arcane. For her role in this affair the Lady deserves a pleasant evening of entertainment, and you will make an admirable escort."

For once, I could make the sharp deduction from the evidence at hand. "You wish me to beg her to forgive you."

"The fair sex is your department, Watson."

An hour later, I departed from our rooms. The rain had ceased, but the clouds remained, and Baker Street was plunged into deep shadows. I looked up at our window and saw Holmes silhouetted against the curtains. What horrible bargain had he made? Were Mycroft and Saint Rita correct, and was my friend's soul in peril? An inexplicable darkness lingered there, as if something were just behind him, waiting to attack.

All my senses urged me to flee.

Yet this was the best and wisest man I had ever known. I clapped my hat on my head and thrust out my chin. No monstrous forces could drive me away, not while Sherlock Holmes needed me.

The Shadows would not prevail.

Author's Note

Once again, as I have borrowed objects, places, and characters from the pages of history, I feel I should give them a moment in the spotlight.

The "Devil's Bible," or *Codex Gigas* (Giant Book) is the largest known medieval manuscript in the world. Thought to have been created in the thirteenth century, the 165-pound volume contains the vulgate Bible, a wealth of historic documents, and a gruesome portrait of Satan. Pilfered from Prague during the Thirty Years War, it is now housed in the National Library of Sweden in Stockholm. And there are indeed some missing pages.

Beneath a church in Palermo are the Capuchin catacombs. The Capuchin brothers began burying members of their order there in the late 1500s, and the unique nature of the vaults helped to naturally mummify and preserve hundreds of bodies. To be entombed in the catacombs became a sign of social status, and people of many different ages and professions were eventually displayed in their final repose. Travelers can visit this macabre attraction, where the last burial was made in the 1920s. I have taken liberties in describing the size of the chambers, but a quick glance online at the pictures of the corpses of monks, soldiers, and young women will confirm why Dr. Watson found them so horrifying.

Born Margherita Lotti in 1381, the woman who would become Saint Rita of Cascia was forced into an arranged marriage with an abusive husband, but persevered to become an example of patience and virtue, discouraging her sons from continuing a feud after their father was murdered. Late in life she experienced a partial stigmata, developing a bleeding wound on her forehead. After her death in 1457, it was noted that her body did not decay, and she remains one of the incorruptible worthies of the Catholic Church. Her body is on display in a shrine in the Basilica of Cascia, where pilgrims continue to seek the intervention of the Patroness of Impossible Causes. Her iconography often features roses and the bees that were said to have gathered at her cradle, hinting at the virtuous life she would live.

A more secular miracle worker was John Nevil Maskelyne, the great London magician. Born in 1839, Maskelyne decided to become a magician after watching a performance by two mediums and realizing that he could duplicate and improve upon their tricks. In partnership with George Alfred Cooke, Maskelyne invented many of the illusions still performed in shows around the world, including levitation (as opposed to suspension), and had a remarkable run as the featured conjurer at the Egyptian Hall in Piccadilly from 1873 to 1904. Like Houdini, Maskelyne was active in debunking the claims of spiritualists. In 1914 Maskelyne founded the Occult Committee, a group charged with investigating the supernatural and exposing frauds. Maskelyne also famously unveiled the secrets of card cheats. Following Cooke's death in 1904, Maskelyne partnered with another rising star of the magic world, David Devant. The Great Maskelyne died in 1917.

On the infamous side of conjuring is Gilles de Rais, more formally known as Gilles de Montmorency-Laval, Baron de Rais. Born around 1405, Rais was a knight and lord who won praise for his courage while fighting alongside Joan of Arc. He retired from military service and quickly alienated his relatives by wasting his money in a series of extravagant theatrical performances. In 1440, the Bishop of Nantes began an investigation of Rais's odd behavior. Rais was arrested and soon confessed to a litany of horrendous deeds, including the rape and murder of young boys as well as devil worship. On October 26, 1440, Rais and two accomplices were executed, their bodies hanged and burned. Rais's charred corpse was given to four noble ladies for burial. The question of his guilt continues to be debated. Most historians hold that he was one of the world's first true serial killers, but some researchers argue that he was the victim of a church inquisition and confessed only to avoid torture and excommunication. Gilles de Rais's alleged murderous habits may have inspired the folktale of Bluebeard. While Bluebeard killed his wives rather than young boys, the image of a wealthy man luring innocents to a castle, only to hang them on hooks, has its echoes in Rais's gruesome confessions.

A better-known figure of depravity is Grigori Yefimovich Rasputin. Born in 1869 in a village in Siberia, this illiterate peasant adopted the life of a religious mystic and by the early 1900s was widely known as a *starnnik* (religious wander) or a *starets* (elder). He developed a reputation for faith healing, which led to his summons to the imperial court of the Romanovs, where the Tsarina Alexandra was desperate for the services of anyone who could keep her hemophiliac son, the Tsesarevich Alexi, alive. Rasputin's presence calmed the boy, leading his mother to grant Rasputin unprecedented access to the royal family and an advisory role that the Russian nobility found inappropriate. Rasputin's other reputation, as a sexual deviant and philanderer, soon discredited him with the Russian people, who were kept unaware of the heir's infirmity. Rumors of perversion at the court led Russians to blame Rasputin for their country's disastrous performance in the First World War and helped to destroy the nation's respect for the imperial family. On December 29, 1916, Prince Felix Yusupov and a small group of conspirators lured Rasputin to the Moika Palace in St. Petersburg and murdered him. Though modern research casts doubt on Yusupov's story---which credited Rasputin with superhuman powers of immunity to cyanide and bullets---Rasputin's assassination was a cruel blow to the Romanovs, who would later be savagely murdered by Bolsheviks during the Russian Civil War.

Perhaps the most famous murder victims in history are the five "canonical" victims of Jack the Ripper, some of whom may have been photographed by the real Joseph Martin. Killed between August 31 and November 9, 1888, Mary Nichols, Annie Chapman, Elizabeth Stride, Catherine Eddowes, and Mary Kelly were all prostitutes in the notorious Whitechapel section of London. Though murder was definitely not new to this slum, the sheer brutality of the killings, and the way all but one body was left to public exposure, caused both fascination and consternation across England. The case remains one of the most investigated and debated of all time. "Ripperologists" are constantly claiming to have solved the crime via historical research and modern forensic methods. However, the true identity of Jack the Ripper remains elusive, known only, perhaps, to Sherlock Holmes....

Also from MX Publishing

MX Publishing is the world's largest specialist Sherlock Holmes publisher, with over a hundred titles and fifty authors creating the latest in Sherlock Holmes fiction and non-fiction.

From traditional short stories and novels to travel guides and quiz books, MX Publishing cater for all Holmes fans.

The collection includes leading titles such as *Benedict Cumberbatch In Transition* and *The Norwood Author* which won the 2011 Howlett Award (Sherlock Holmes Book of the Year).

MX Publishing also has one of the largest communities of Holmes fans on Facebook with regular contributions from dozens of authors.

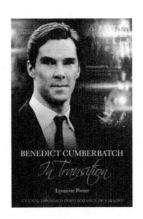

www.mxpublishing.com